'Thanks for the lift,' Julia said, slamming the door behind her with unnecessary vigour, but Nathan caught up to her before she could undo the catch on the garden gate.

'I'm coming in with you,' he said, taking her arm in a firm grip and propelling her along the path to the front door.

'No, you are *not* coming in with me!'

'All I want to do is talk to you, and there is absolutely no reason for you to behave like a petrified virgin in fear of being raped. It's ten-thirty,' he said abruptly, glancing at the gold watch strapped to his lean wrist. 'I doubt that you would have complained had Warren Chandler kept you out this late.'

She stiffened at that hint of mockery in his voice. 'I happen to enjoy Warren's company.'

'Meaning you don't enjoy mine?'

TOO LONG A SACRIFICE

BY

YVONNE WHITTAL

MILLS & BOON LIMITED
ETON HOUSE   18-24 PARADISE ROAD
RICHMOND   SURREY   TW9 1SR

*First published in Great Britain 1988
by Mills & Boon Limited*

© Yvonne Whittal 1988

*Australian copyright 1988
Philippine copyright 1988
This edition 1988*

ISBN 0 263 76002 2

*Set in English Times 10 on 11 pt.
01–0688–41037*

Typeset in Great Britain by JCL Graphics, Bristol

*Printed and bound in Great Britain by
Collins, Glasgow*

CHAPTER ONE

THE waiting-room had been packed with patients waiting to see the doctor that Saturday morning, and the fan whirring on the filing-cabinet had fought a losing battle to circulate the air in the room. It was January in southern Africa when the summer was at its peak, and the northern Transvaal was noted for its sweltering heat, but Julia Henderson succeeded in projecting an image of cool, calm professionalism in her white nurse's uniform.

Sophie Breedt was the last patient in the waiting-room at twelve thirty. She was a woman well into her sixties with grey hair combed back into a neat, old-fashioned bun in the nape of her neck. Her ample figure was ensconced in an armchair and, when she looked up to find Julia's glance resting on her, she closed the magazine she had been paging through and placed it on the table beside her chair.

'I've sold Honeywell,' she said chattily, but there was a deep sadness in her watery hazel eyes. 'George and I never had any children and there is no point in staying on alone at the farm now that he is no longer alive.'

Julia Henderson's greatest problem as a nursing sister had always been her inability to distance herself from the suffering of others, and her grey glance clouded with sympathy and concern when this woman's pain became her own.

'Where will you go?' she asked the woman whom everyone in Doornfield knew as Tant Sophie.

'My sister is also a widow, and she has invited me to stay with her at Potgietersrus for a while.' There was a hint of

5

despair in the vague gesture she made with her plump hands. 'If I like it there then I might buy a small place of my own later.'

'Have you sold the farm to someone local?' Julia asked the older woman conversationally, while she closed the appointment book and began to straighten her desk.

'No, I sold it to a doctor from Johannesburg who made me a better offer than anyone else in the district.' Tant Sophie frowned in concentration. 'I haven't met the man, but I think my lawyer said his name was Nathan Corbett.'

Nathan Corbett! Julia reeled mentally as if she had been dealt a vicious blow, and the blood drained from her face to leave her chalk-white. There could not be more than one Nathan Corbett in the medical profession, and the name alone conjured up memories which were still too painful to dwell on. She had thought that they would never meet again, but for some obscure reason fate was bringing him here to Doornfield.

'You look ill,' Sophie Breedt was saying as if from a great distance away. 'Are you feeling faint?'

Julia took a deep, steadying breath and made a supreme effort to pull herself together. 'No, I'm fine.'

'It's this terrible heat,' said Tant Sophie, placing her own interpretation on the cause of Julia's paleness. 'It took me years to get used to this bushveld heat.'

A pregnant young woman emerged from the consulting-room. Her appearance created a mild diversion, and it gave Julia those extra few seconds to regain complete control of herself before she rose behind her desk with Sophie Breedt's file in her hands.

'You may go in now, Tant Sophie,' she announced, her feelings carefully hidden behind an outwardly calm expression as she held out her hand to help the older woman out of the chair.

Julia's temples were pounding when the consulting-room door closed behind Sophie Breedt's ample figure, but she sat down behind her desk and tried to concentrate on the things she still had to do before she could go home to her safe little cottage on the outskirts of the town.

Safe? The word mocked her ruthlessly. How safe was she going to be with Nathan Corbett owning a farm in the district?

Roland de Necker, in his early fifties and greying swiftly, emerged from his consulting-room half an hour later, and Sophie Breedt was clinging to his arm as if she was reluctant to let go of the man who had been her doctor and her friend for so many years. She said a tearful goodbye, and Julia had a lump in her throat when she followed the elderly doctor back into his consulting-room where he slumped into the leather armchair behind his desk.

'It's been quite a morning,' he sighed tiredly, taking off his gold-rimmed spectacles and cleaning them vigorously with his white linen handkerchief before he put them on again, and gestured Julia into the chair. His green gaze settled on her rigidly controlled features and his mouth tightened. 'I presume you have already heard the news that Sophie Breedt has sold her farm.'

Julia stared down at her clenched hands in her lap. 'Yes, she told me.'

'There is no reason to believe that the man who has bought Honeywell is the same Nathan Corbett you used to know.'

The corners of her soft mouth lifted in a mirthless smile. 'There can't be more than one Nathan Corbett in the medical profession.'

'I imagine that's true,' grunted Roland de Necker, drumming his fingers on the arm of his chair. 'You're not going to do something foolish such as running away, are you?'

'The reason why I ran away once before no longer exists.'

Her grey eyes clouded with memories which still had the power to hurt her to some extent, and Roland got up and circled his desk to place a comforting hand on her shoulder.

'I admire you for laying your own happiness on the sacrificial altar, but there is such a thing as making too long a sacrifice,' he warned, his fingers tightening on her shoulder as if to stress his statement. 'You have been with me for almost three years, and in all this time you have never allowed another man near you. You have shut off your feelings so securely that one day, when you choose to open the door to your heart, you might find nothing there worth giving to someone else.'

Her throat was too tight to speak, and she placed her hand briefly over his where it rested on her shoulder as an indication that she had heard and understood what he had said. Roland de Necker and his wife had been good friends, and she appreciated his concern.

It was not quite true that no other man had been allowed to get close to her. There was Warren Chandler, whose friendship meant a great deal to her. After her arrival in Doornfield she had declined all invitations simply because she had felt that none of the men had matched up to Nathan, and later she had found herself admitting to a general lack of interest. Warren Chandler had persisted, and he had become a friend in whose company she could relax without fearing that he might make certain emotional and physical demands on her.

Julia knew a sudden sense of alarm. She had always imagined herself married and with a family of her own at the age of twenty-seven. The importance of that desire had diminished over the years, and she could almost say that she was content and happy on her own. Was it possible that, as Roland had said, she had already made too long a sacrifice?

She thrust these disturbing thoughts aside when she left the consulting-rooms with Roland de Necker and drove herself home in her white Toyota.

Jacaranda trees lined the almost deserted main street, and flowers in window boxes had wilted in the heat of the sun. This was bushveld country, and Doornfield was a quiet, unpretentious little village situated in the heart of it. Progress and industry had almost passed it by until they had started delving for coal four years ago on an open tract of land ten kilometres out of town. The influx of miners and their families had necessitated the erection of a school and a well equipped hospital, but the peace and tranquillity had somehow remained undisturbed.

Julia reduced her speed to a crawl as she negotiated her car on to the narrow lane which led to her cottage. The gravel lane continued past her cottage, curving and twisting down among the tall bluegum trees towards the river where the local residents occasionally spent their weekends angling in the rushing waters, or picnicking beneath the shady trees.

She unlocked the door of her thatch-roofed cottage a few minutes later, and walked down the short passage to her bedroom where she flung her handbag on her bed and kicked off her shoes. There was peace in her surroundings, but there was no peace in her heart at that moment as she turned towards the dressing-table and pulled the combs from her honey-brown hair to let it cascade in glossy waves on to her shoulders.

Have I changed much? she wondered as she unintentionally appraised herself in the mirror. Candid grey eyes stared back at her from beneath attractively arched brows. Her nose was small and straight, and there was an upward tilt at the corners of her wide, generous mouth which suggested that she smiled easily. Her glance became somewhat critical when she studied her figure. She had lost a considerable amount of weight five years ago, and she had regained very little of it, but her slender body had lost none of its resilience.

Julia did not linger in front of the mirror, and even if she had she would not have noticed the appealing beauty of her fine-boned features. There was strength in the firmness of her chin, and a natural grace in the way her supple body moved, but she was not aware of this as she went to the kitchen to make herself a cup of tea.

She was tired, and she felt clammy beneath the spotless white uniform when she filled the electric kettle and switched it on. She drew aside the curtains to stare out of the window, but she did not see the vegetable garden she had cultivated with such care, neither did she see the rocky hills shimmering in the heat beyond the river. The door had been slammed securely on her past, but Sophie Breedt had wrenched it open with her disclosure, and Julia could no longer curb the memories that spilled out into her mind.

She had met Nathan Corbett on a date which had been arranged by Damian Squires, a mutual friend in the medical profession. Julia had been attracted to Nathan at first because of his outward appearance. He was tall, with dark hair which had a tendency to curl on to his broad forehead, and he had the bluest eyes she had ever seen. Later she had liked him for very different reasons. He had not made an issue of the fact that, at thirty, he was a qualified neuro-surgeon, while she was a junior theatre sister. He had been eight years her senior, but Julia had been able to talk to him in a way in which she had never been able to talk to any other man. He had a quick mind, and a sharp, sometimes stinging wit which had appealed to her intellect. She had found him both bracing and challenging to be with, and it had perhaps been inevitable that she should eventually fall in love with him.

They had been engaged to be married when Nathan was offered the opportunity to spend four years working with some of Europe's most eminent neuro-surgeons, and it had been an opportunity which he could not afford to reject. Their wedding date had been brought forward so that Julia could accompany him, but, with less than a month to go before their wedding and subsequent departure for Europe, fate stepped in to alter the course of their lives.

The whistle on the electric kettle went off like a siren, jolting Julia back to the present, and for a few minutes she busied herself making a small pot of tea, but the memories of the past came rushing back to the fore when she sat down at the well scrubbed wooden table with her cup of tea in front of her.

She did not think that she would ever forget the day when she was told that her grandmother had cancer. The doctor had given Alicia Henderson a year to live, and, with special treatment, perhaps two or three. Julia had suddenly found herself in a position where she had to make the most difficult decision of her life. She had loved Nathan, and she had desperately wanted to marry him, but she could not go away with him and leave the woman who had reared her almost from infancy after the tragic death of her parents.

Julia drank her tea and tried to relax, but those long-buried memories would give her no peace, and she was forced to recall those last few weeks in Johannesburg before Nathan's departure for Europe. She had been forced to make a traumatic decision, and if Nathan had noticed anything different about her, then he had not mentioned it. The problem was, perhaps, that she had

known him too well. If she had told him the truth he
might have forfeited the opportunity to go to Europe in
order to stay with her, but Julia had known that she
could not allow him to sacrifice his career for her sake.
Nathan was destined for greater heights in his
profession as a neuro-surgeon, and her *mind,* if not her
heart, had told her that *she* was the one who would have
to make the sacrifice.

She felt the perspiration break out on her forehead at
the memory of her predicament. She had been incapable
of facing Nathan and saying the words which she knew
had to be said. He would have known that she was
lying, and she had had to resort to writing him a letter.
It had taken her days to compose something which she
had hoped would ease the hurt for him, but in the end
she had realised that there was no nice way of breaking
off their engagement, and she had severed their
relationship in a few brief words which had sliced deep
into her own soul. She had added her engagement ring
to the letter in the envelope, she had sealed it carefully,
and she had had it delivered by hand to Nathan's rooms
in the city, but, by the time he received it, she had left
Johannesburg with her grandmother on a holiday from
which they did not return until she had heard that
Nathan had left the country.

That had been five years ago, and Damian Squires
was the only one who had known the truth. He had been
someone she could trust, someone she could confide in,
and she had known that he would never reveal her secret
to anyone who might unwittingly pass it on to Nathan.

Alicia Henderson had lived a little more than two
years and, after her death, Julia had sold the house
which had been her home for so many years. She had
wanted to get away, and Doornfield had seemed the
ideal place at the time. She had needed to regain an

inner peace, and the tranquillity of this small town had given her that . . . and more.

Julia poured herself a second cup of tea and got up to fetch the headache tablets which she always kept in the kitchen dresser. Her head was throbbing, and she gulped down two tablets with a mouthful of tea.

There was nothing strange about Nathan's buying a farm. Many professional men possessed farms these days, and they used them as a retreat from their pressurised lives in the city, but fate had in some diabolical way guided Nathan to choose the Doornfield district in which to buy a farm. Why? Oh, God, *why?* It *had* to be sheer coincidence. No one would have told him where she lived; Damian would have kept her secret, and there was also no reason to suspect that Nathan would go to any great length to meet her again. Not after what she had done to him.

Dear God, she had had no choice! Nathan did not know that, and she wondered what his feelings were when he thought of her. *If* he ever thought about her.

Julia changed into an old pair of slacks and a faded T-shirt. Her headache was subsiding, and she had always found it therapeutic to work in her small garden. Barefoot, and with a dilapidated old straw hat planted firmly on her head, she went down on to her knees in her flower garden to loosen the soil between the seedlings she had planted a week ago.

She worked steadily for more than an hour before she went inside to pour herself a glass of fruit juice which she took out into the garden with her. She seated herself on one of the garden chairs which stood in a shady spot, and she drank thirstily from her glass while she glanced about her appreciatively.

The lawn was green, but the edges needed to be trimmed again. At the farthest end of the small garden the poinsettia was blooming, its flowers a brilliant scarlet in the sunshine. Beside the gate the hibiscus was flowering, and her pink and yellow roses were ranked in profusion along the low picket fence. The cottage was small with whitewashed walls and green shutters at the windows which were more decorative than functional.

It presented a peaceful picture, and Julia began to relax at last. It was silly to get herself into a panic about Nathan, she told herself eventually. The fact that he had bought Honeywell did not necessarily mean that they would be bumping into each other at every turn. It was quite possible that he might never even discover that she was living in Doornfield. He was, after all, not going to take up permanent residence on the farm. Was he?

Despite all her efforts to the contrary, Julia lacked her usual calm during the ensuing weeks. Sophie Breedt's departure from Doornfield had aroused an anxiety in Julia which made her quake inwardly every time her telephone rang at the cottage and, when she did her shopping in town, she could not prevent herself from glancing repeatedly over her shoulder as if she expected to see Nathan coming up behind her.

'You haven't been quite yourself these past few weeks,' Roland de Necker commented over a cup of tea one Friday morning before the expected rush of patients.

'I didn't think it showed that much.'

'I doubt if anyone else has noticed, but I happen to know you better than you think.' He observed her intently from behind his gold-rimmed spectacles. 'It's Nathan Corbett, isn't it?'

Julia nodded and smiled self-consciously. 'I have this unreasonable fear that I'm going to turn a corner and bump into him.'

'Are you afraid of him in particular, or are you afraid of yourself?'

'I think a little of both,' she admitted, placing her empty cup in the tray on Roland's desk. 'I'm afraid of what he might do and say, and I'm not at all sure how I shall react if we should meet again.'

'Forewarned is forearmed,' Roland pointed out, 'and Nathan doesn't have that advantage.'

'I'm not so sure that being forewarned is such a wonderful advantage,' she smiled with unaccustomed cynicism. 'If I hadn't known about Nathan buying Sophie Breedt's farm, then I wouldn't have been in this state of anxiety about a meeting which I'm beginning to suspect is predestined.'

Roland frowned and pushed out his lower lip in characteristic thoughtfulness, then he changed the subject abruptly. 'I hope you haven't planned anything in particular for this coming Sunday.'

'What's happening on Sunday?' she asked warily.

'You're invited to lunch.' His green gaze sparkled with amusement when she relaxed visibly. 'Elizabeth is in the mood to roast a leg of lamb, and we need someone to help us eat it.'

'Elizabeth always does a marvellous roast, and nothing on this earth is going to prevent me from sharing it with you.' Julia smiled at him and shifted her fears and problems aside for the moment. 'Thank you for the invitation, and tell Elizabeth that I gladly accept.'

The shrill ringing of the telephone interrupted them, and Roland de Necker got up to follow Julia when she went into the waiting-room to answer it.

'It's Sister Murray from maternity,' she informed him with her hand over the mouthpiece. 'Mrs Jenson is in the final stages of labour.'

'Tell her I'm on my way,' he said, striding briskly into his consulting-room to collect his stethoscope and car keys.

Julia passed on Roland's message, and he had already left the building when she replaced the receiver.

The rest of the day was hectic as usual. Roland was delayed at the hospital, and Julia had her hands full coping with patients who were becoming irate at having to wait beyond the specified time of their appointments. It was on days such as these that she was thankful for the ability to remain calm and unruffled, but her calmness seemed to desert her when she arrived at her cottage that evening. Alone, and with too much time on her hands, she found her disturbing thoughts returned to haunt her, and she spent yet another restless night wishing for the dawn when she could find forgetfulness in her work.

The de Necker home was spacious and tastefully furnished. The atmosphere was homely, and Elizabeth had prepared a magnificent Sunday lunch which had left Julia feeling lethargic when they retired to the air-conditioned living-room with their tea. The conversation was not taxing, and Roland actually nodded off in his chair until he was called out to the hospital midway through the afternoon. Julia decided it was time she left as well, but Elizabeth seemed reluctant to let her go.

'Stay and have another cup of tea with me,' she invited, and Julia found that she did not need to be coaxed to linger a while longer in her hostess's charming company.

Elizabeth de Necker was a few years younger than her husband, but her fair hair cleverly disguised the fact that she was greying at the temples, and her slender

body still had an enviable youthfulness about it. She
was also a relaxing person to be with, and her warm,
friendly manner had reached out to Julia from their
very first meeting almost three years ago. Elizabeth and
her husband were also the only two people in
Doornfield who knew the reason behind Julia's decision
to start a new life away from Johannesburg. Julia had
taken them into her confidence a long time ago and, like
true friends, the subject had never been mentioned
again. Until now!

'Please don't be offended,' Elizabeth broached the
subject with endearing caution when they were alone
and drinking their tea, 'but wherever I seem to go these
days people are talking about Honeywell's new owner.'

'I know.' Julia smiled stiffly and gazed down into her
teacup. 'I've heard them talking and speculating in the
consulting-rooms.'

'How do you feel about it?'

Julia did not need time to consider Elizabeth's query,
and she answered her with inherent honesty. 'It scares
me knowing that there's a possibility Nathan and I
might meet again in the near future.'

Elizabeth nodded with understanding, but her brown
eyes were thoughtful and intent upon Julia's face when
she asked, 'Are you still in love with him?'

Julia had not yet dared to ask herself that question
during all the restless hours she had spent fretting about
the possibility of meeting Nathan again, but suddenly
she was startled into taking a moment to consider her
feelings. Was she still in love with Nathan?

'I wish I could give you a precise "yes" or "no"
answer, but I can't,' she confessed at length, rising to
place her empty cup in the tray and walking towards the
window to stare blindly out across the sun-washed
garden with its colourful array of shrubs and flowers.

'I knew five years ago that I had to shut him out of my life, and I've been working at it ever since. I would be lying if I said that I've never thought about him. I've thought about him often, but always with the knowledge that he belonged to my past, and to have him suddenly thrust into my present is something that really frightens me.'

'Are you afraid you might find that you still love him?'

'I'm not sure what I'm afraid of,' Julia replied candidly, turning to face Elizabeth with a frown marring her smooth brow. 'I had to make a decision five years ago which hurt me as much as I imagine it must have hurt him, but I don't regret my decision, and I'm consoled by the knowledge that my motives were sincere. I couldn't leave my grandmother when I knew that she was dying and needed me, and I did what I considered was best for Nathan at the time, but I have a feeling that he won't see it that way.' Her small hands fluttered in a despairing gesture. 'What is a man supposed to think and feel a few days before his wedding when he receives an unexpected letter telling him that the girl he was going to marry no longer loves him?'

'I should imagine he would be hurt and angry, but I'm sure that he would eventually be determined to discover the reason for her change of heart,' Elizabeth answered her soberly and logically, but her attractive features brightened the next instant with an animated smile. 'Consider the possibilities, Julia. You will at last have the opportunity to explain the reasons behind your actions, and who knows what might happen after that.'

'I like your optimism, Elizabeth,' Julia smiled wryly as she returned to her chair, 'but I don't somehow think it's going to be *that* easy.'

'Why shouldn't it be easy?' demanded Elizabeth.

'First, because this is all pure conjecture,' Julia pointed out rationally. 'Second, Nathan always was a man with a great deal of pride. He might still forgive me for hurting his feelings, but I doubt if he will ever forgive me for hurting his pride.' Julia could feel her body grow taut with tension while she spoke, and she lowered her gaze to her hands which she had clasped together so tightly in her lap that her fingers had begun to ache. 'And last but not least,' she added quietly, 'it would be foolish to overlook the fact that he might be happily married, and not at all interested in whatever explanation I might want to give him.'

'Whatever happens, Julia,' Elizabeth remarked after a lengthy silence, 'I'm sure it will be for the best.'

Their conversation ended on that note, and Julia left soon afterwards to return to her cottage.

Children played in the park alongside the municipal offices. Julia could hear their shrill, excited voices as she drove past, and she could not help wishing that she was a child again. Childhood had been such a carefree time for her, but growing up had meant facing problems and making decisions, and she had not always found solace in the conviction that she had made the right choice.

Julia drove on through the quiet streets. There was no sense in speculating about what she might have done if she had to have her life over again, and she sighed heavily when she finally turned off on to the narrow lane which led to the river.

She reduced speed and changed down to a low gear to drive slowly past the row of familiar cottages. She was nearing the final bend in the lane when a red, low-slung vehicle appeared as if from nowhere directly ahead of her, and it was bearing down on her at breakneck speed. There was no time for contemplation, she had to avoid a collision, and she reacted instinctively. She turned sharply to the left, steering her Toyota into a shallow ditch at the side of the lane as the red monster skimmed past her, but the next instant she had to step hard on the brake to bring her car to a shuddering halt inches from the broad stem of a gum tree. The Toyota's engine cut out, and the deafening silence which followed was disturbed only by the thudding pace of her own heartbeats.

It had all happened so quickly that there had been no time for thought. It was over in one terrifying instant and, too numb with shock to wonder at the identity of the careless driver, she buried her face in her arms on the steering-wheel. She did not hear the footsteps approaching her car at a brisk pace, and she was still sitting with her head bowed on her arms when the door was wrenched open beside her.

A hand touched her shoulder, and a brisk, professional voice was asking, 'Did you hurt yourself? Are you in pain?'

A renewed wave of shock rippled through Julia, and it felt curiously as if the air was being drained from her lungs. The deep, resonant timbre of that voice was too familiar ever to forget, she would know it anywhere even if she lived to be a hundred, and she had no option but to raise her head and look up into that equally familiar face so close to her own.

Nathan Corbett's hand released her shoulder as if he had come into contact with a leprous object, and his surprise was evident when he stepped back a pace, but he controlled himself with admirable swiftness, his ruggedly handsome features settling into a cold and impenetrable mask that sent a shiver of apprehension racing along her spine.

'Well, it's a small world, isn't it,' he commented

with a biting sarcasm that made her wince inwardly, and she could feel herself shrinking beneath the probing intensity of his clinical glance. 'Are you hurt?'

Her mouth felt dry, and she swallowed convulsively before she shook her head and croaked, 'No, I'm all right.'

'What the *hell* are you doing here in Doornfield?'

The past washed over her in one painful wave after the other while she sat there staring at him a little stupidly with her clammy hands clamped about the steering-wheel. At first glance he had not changed much except for the deepening of the grooves which ran from his high-bridged nose down to the corners of his strong, sensuous mouth, and he still had the bluest eyes she had ever seen, but they were flint-hard when they met hers, making him a harsh, formidable stranger.

'I happen to live here,' she heard herself explaining in a voice which sounded quite unlike her own. 'My cottage is the last one before the road curves down to the river.'

'Is everything all right, darling?'

Julia glanced over her shoulder at the sound of that feminine voice, and her insides jolted savagely when she saw a dark-haired woman emerge from the driver's seat of the Ferrari which had been parked a short distance away. Was this Nathan's wife? Julia wondered as she watched the woman walk towards them in her baggy yellow slacks and equally baggy red blouse which had been girded in at her slender waist with a red and yellow polka-dot sash. This woman was dressed youthfully, but Julia guessed that she was not as young as she intended everyone to believe.

'Everything is under control,' Nathan replied, and Julia was suffused with the desire to laugh out loud.

Everything is under control! Oh, God, if only that

were true! Shock was suddenly taking its toll. Her emotions were in a frantic, unrecognisable turmoil, and she was shaking so much that she had no idea how she was going to drive the short distance to her cottage. She also had a dreadful feeling that she was going to burst into hysterical tears at any moment, and she wished that Nathan would go away and leave her alone.

'This really is a poor excuse for a road, and I can only say it's a miracle that no one was hurt,' Nathan's lady-friend remarked when she reached his side, and her dark gaze sharpened unexpectedly when it rested on Julia.

'Marcia, this is Julia.' Nathan introduced them without so much as a flicker of emotion on his rugged face, and the casualness of his introduction made Julia suspect that he had taken Marcia into his confidence.

The atmosphere was all at once crackling with tension as Julia received a cool, wordless nod in greeting, and she responded in a similar manner while she withstood the calculating stare of those dark, almond-shaped eyes. Marcia was an extremely beautiful woman, but Julia sensed a hard inner core which suggested a sad lack of warmth and compassion.

'We really must hurry, darling, if we're to be at the farm before our visitors arrive,' Marcia reminded Nathan impatiently, and she ignored Julia as she linked her arm through his in a possessive gesture which said quite clearly, *'He belongs to me now!'*

A look of indecision flashed across Nathan's face, but Julia's nerves were fast approaching breaking-point.

'Please don't let me delay you,' she said stiffly, turning the key in the ignition, and sighing inwardly with relief when the Toyota's engine sprang to life.

Nathan closed the door without speaking, and they stepped away from her car as she reversed out of the ditch. Julia slammed the gear lever into first, let in the clutch, and drove on down the lane without daring to look back.

CHAPTER TWO

JULIA could not recall afterwards how she had succeeded in garaging her car without a mishap when she arrived at the cottage. She was shaken to the core, and she had entered her bedroom like an automaton to lie face-down on her bed. It had taken a long time for those terrible tremors to subside inside her, and afterwards she had been left with an uneasy feeling that she had not seen the last of Nathan Corbett. She had known that meeting him again after all this time might be an ordeal, but the shock of their near collision in the lane had shattered her calm, and it had very nearly snapped her rigid control.

She forced herself to eat and drink something before she went to bed, but she slept very little that night, and she awoke the following morning with a head that felt twice its normal size. She had wondered for weeks how she would feel if she had to see Nathan again, but when she analysed her feelings that morning she could recall only the shock and the near-hysteria.

'You've been looking a little peaky all morning,' Roland remarked after lunch that day when he was free for a few minutes to have a cup of tea with Julia, and his clinical glance lingered intently on her hollow-eyed face. 'You look as if you didn't sleep very well last night. Aren't you feeling well?'

'I had a bad night, but I'm not ill,' Julia assured him, draining her cup and placing it in the tray on his desk. 'I met Nathan very briefly yesterday afternoon after I left your house.'

Roland's eyebrows rose in a query behind his gold-rimmed spectacles, and she felt compelled to explain briefly what had occurred.

'Do you think Nathan is married to this Marcia woman?' Roland asked when she fell silent, and Julia shrugged.

'I have no idea.'

Roland drummed his fingers absently on the arm of his chair and frowned. 'I've heard from a reliable source that Nathan sent a crew of interior decorators up ahead of him to renovate the old house on the farm, and it seems as if he has plans to spend the next six weeks at Honeywell.'

Julia did not question Roland about his source of information, but her uneasiness increased at the knowledge that Nathan would be spending the next six weeks on the farm. Doornfield had suddenly become too small to accommodate both Nathan and herself, and she was not looking forward to a second meeting.

'Don't leap ahead at problems which might never arise, Julia,' Roland advised as if he had gauged her thoughts and fears. 'Take each day as it comes, and deal with each problem *if* and *when* it arises.'

Julia appreciated his advice, and she had cause to remember it when she arrived home late one afternoon later that week to see that now familiar red Ferrari parked outside her gate. Her body grew tense, and her heart leapt uncomfortably in her breast a few seconds later when she had garaged her car to find Nathan standing a short distance from her beside a wooden arch on which a lilac bougainvillaea was growing profusely.

'I thought your grandmother would have moved up here to live with you.'

Julia stared at him for a moment, taking in the blue

denims fitting snugly across his lean hips and muscular thighs, and the white, sleeveless T-shirt with the V-neck which gave her more than a glimpse of the short dark hair curling against his tanned chest. A pulse began to throb frantically at the base of her throat. It made her realise that she was not as unaffected by his presence as she would have wished to be, and she looked away again hastily.

'My grandmother died three years ago,' Julia informed him matter-of-factly, stepping past him to walk along the concrete path to her front door, and her nerves coiled into a knot at the pit of her stomach at the knowledge that he was following her.

'I'm sorry to hear that,' he was saying. 'I remember her as a strong, robust woman who was seldom ill, and I find it difficult to believe that she isn't still alive.'

Julia's thoughts were too chaotic to speak, and she needed those few moments to control her features as well as her erratic heart-beats while she unlocked the door, but Nathan was observing her with a faintly sardonic expression in his blue eyes when she turned to face him.

'May I come in, Julia?'

She hesitated nervously. She did not welcome the thought of being alone with him, but common sense warned that he might suspect she was afraid of him, and she pushed open the door, entering the small cottage ahead of him with a cool, 'You may come in, if you wish.'

Julia led the way into her small lounge with its comfortable cane furniture, and she was aware of Nathan glancing about him while she deposited her handbag and her parcels on the chair nearest to her. His glance seemed to take in every detail of the bright floral cushions, the plain cream curtains which were drawn aside at the window to let in the late afternoon sun, and the wall unit which contained her hi-fi and a small television set.

Nathan sauntered towards the stand containing her collection of classical records, and she felt awkwardly tense and uneasy when he lingered there to glance through them. Why was he here? What was he looking for? And what did he hope to find?

'I see you still have the same taste in music,' he smiled twistedly when he turned unexpectedly and caught her in the act of observing him. 'That, at least, is something that hasn't changed.'

The accusation in his remark did not escape her. He was referring to what he considered was the inconstancy of her emotions all those years ago, and she was surprised to discover that it hurt, but she was determined not to let it show.

'Why are you here, Nathan?'

'I came to find out if you perhaps have a husband tucked away somewhere, but you're not wearing any rings, so I presume that you're still single.' His smile deepened with derision. 'What's the matter, Julia? Don't you have the guts to take a relationship through to the final commitment of marriage?'

She lowered her lashes to veil the pain in her eyes. 'Is this going to be an inquisition?'

'I'm merely curious,' he drawled mockingly, raising a hand to straighten the original landscape against the wall which had always hung in her grandmother's house, but his cold blue gaze seemed to pin her helplessly to the floor when he turned abruptly. 'Why did you leave Johannesburg? Was the emotional climate getting too hot for you? Did you leave too many prospective husbands dangling a few days before the wedding to stay on in the city?'

Julia had been prepared for something like this, and she had known that it was not going to be an easy confrontation. His anger was understandable; it was a natural reaction, but she had been unprepared for the near physical pain as each word he uttered stabbed savagely at her heart.

'If you have come here to insult me, then I suggest you leave before I lose my temper,' she said calmly, hiding her feelings with an adroitness which had taken her five years to perfect almost to a fine art.

'I didn't know you had a temper,' he mocked her, increasing her heart-wrenching awareness of the change in him from the man she had once known to the man she was now confronted with. 'Perhaps I ought to congratulate you on your ability to keep that as well as every other part of your character hidden so well,' he added with a biting sarcasm she had not known he possessed and, when she did not answer him, he raised one dark, cynical eyebrow. 'Do you have nothing to say to that?'

What could she say in her own defence? He was searching for whatever whip he could lay his hands on in order to thrash her, and she could not blame him entirely.

'I've had a tough day, Nathan,' she said coolly, her glance unwavering even while her hands clutched at the backrest of the chair in front of her to steady her trembling body. 'Do you think you could explain the reason for this visit?'

He hooked his thumbs in the pockets of his denims, and he lessened the distance between them, giving her that half-forgotten feeling that she had shrunk from average height to the size of a dwarf. Her eyes were almost on a level with the deep V of his T-shirt where the dark hair curled against his chest. It evoked haunting memories of leisurely picnics at the Hartebeespoort dam, and of lying in his arms with her cheek resting against his warm skin.

Dear God! She must not think about the past! And, above all, she must not think about what this man had once meant to her!

'I want to know why you left Johannesburg,' he demanded in a quiet, authoritative voice, his compelling glance drawing hers and holding it relentlessly while she tried to control her emotions.

'I didn't want to stay on after my grandmother died, so I sold the house and decided to settle here,' she answered him, relieved that she did not have to lie about that, and she decided to risk a query of her own while she had the opportunity. 'What made you decide to buy a farm in this district?'

'I heard from someone who had heard from someone else that there was a farm for sale in the Doornfield district, and I badly need a place I can excape to when the pressure of work becomes too much.' His eyes narrowed speculatively. 'Why are you working as a doctor's receptionist/nurse when you are better qualified for hospital duty?'

'It was the only job I could get when I came here three years ago, and I have stayed on because I am happy working for Dr de Necker.' Nathan's nearness and the familiar scent of his masculine cologne were attacking her senses, and Julia moved away from him towards the door. 'Would you like a cup of coffee,' she offered politely, 'or are you in a hurry to return to you . . . er . . . wife?'

'I'd like a cup of coffee,' he said, his mouth twitching with a suggestion of a smile when she faltered, but his eyes remained cold and assessing. 'Marcia left early this afternoon to return to Johannesburg with our guests, and she isn't my wife.'

'Oh?' Julia did not quite know how she felt about the news that Nathan was not married to Marcia. She would analyse her feelings later, she decided, when she turned in the doorway to look at him, and she noticed, not for the first time, that his hair still had a tendency to curl on to his broad forehead. 'She's your fiancée, then?' she heard herself asking before she could prevent herself.

'We haven't got around to that yet.' The atmosphere was inexplicably tense, while his glance held hers with a steady, probing regard.

Julia felt the shock of his words like a sickening blow to the heart, and it left her pale and momentarily speechless. What did it matter? she asked herself with some annoyance. She had not expected him to remain faithful to her, and neither had she expected him to live the life of a celibate after the way she had practically jilted him on the eve of their wedding. Had she? *No, of course not!* she answered her own question rationally. But why did it have to hurt so much? She had got over her feelings for him a long time ago, hadn't she?

'I'll switch on the kettle,' she said, her voice sounding as hollow as she was feeling at that moment when she turned from him with a jerky movement and escaped into the kitchen.

Julia drew aside the curtains at the window, and she filled the electric kettle under the tap before she plugged it into the wall and switched it on. She was functioning automatically, taking down two cups and saucers out of the wall cupboard and spooning instant coffee into them. Her thoughts were in a turmoil, and her feelings were in an equally chaotic state. She clenched her hands where they rested on the cupboard, and she clamped her jaw so tightly that the muscles in her cheeks ached. Nathan was free to live his life as he wished, and so was *she!* What did it matter to her that he and Marcia were lovers?

Her nerves jarred violently at the sound of a step behind her, and she took a moment to control her features before she turned to find Natha observing her from no more than a pace away. There was a gleam of mockery in his eyes, and it sent an embarrassing warmth rushing into her cheeks.

'Have I shocked your puritanical little mind?' he demanded, the deep timbre of his voice ringing with the mockery she had seen in his eyes, and unaccustomed anger came to her rescue.

'I'm well aware of the fact that promiscuity is no longer frowned upon in our modern society, but I must warn you to tread with care if you wish to gain the respect of the Doornfield locals.' The kettle whistled loudly while she spoke, and she switched it off at the wall, praying that the tremor in her hand would go unnoticed when she poured boiling water into their cups and added milk. 'The people of importance in this village are all descendants of pioneers, and they still harbour the old-fashioned notion that a man takes a woman to bed *after* he has married her.'

'You sound as if you care about my reputation,' he mocked her, his short bark of derisive laughter making her anger rise by several degrees, and her grey glance was stormy when she handed him his cup of coffee and brushed past him to return the carton of milk to the refrigerator.

'The rise and fall of your reputation is *your* concern, Nathan, and I merely considered it my duty to enlighten you as to the moral code by which most people live here in Doornfield,' she assured him coldly, the limited space in her kitchen forcing her to squeeze past him again to add sugar to her own cup, and she was uncomfortably aware of his razor-sharp eyes following every move she was making. 'Shall we take our coffee through to the lounge?'

Nathan's rugged features were set in a hard, unfathomable mask when he stood aside for her to precede him out of the kitchen, and he followed disturbingly close behind her. She could feel his eyes boring into her back, and she sighed inwardly with a measure of relief when they were seated facing each other to drink their coffee, but her relief was short-lived. The silence between Nathan and herself was uncomfortable, and fraught with a strange tension which seemed to take a painful hold of every muscle in her body. He was studying her intently over the rim of his cup, his glance narrowed and assessing as it trailed from her honey-brown hair coiled into a neat knot in the nape of her neck, down to the sensible, low-heeled shoes on her feet, and a disquieting sensation spiralled through her to restrict her breathing.

'Talking about morals,' he said at length, referring to the conversation they had had in the kitchen and making her heart skip a frightened beat. She watched him down the last of his coffee, and she was unnerved by the cynical smile curving his sensuous mouth when he leaned forward to place his cup on the circular glass coffee-table. 'Isn't there something in your book of moral codes that says a man deserves a reasonable explanation why the woman he was going to marry should suddenly change her mind at the very last minute?'

Julia had expected this, but his query still had the power to shake her, and she had to take a few moments to gather her scattered wits about her. She was painfully aware of the fact that she would have to exercise extreme caution. One carelessly chosen word could set him on the trail of his quest for the truth, but the truth would no longer serve a purpose and, for her own sake, it had to remain hidden from him.

'I believe I said everything there was to say in my letter to you,' she answered him coolly and with a calmness which she was far from experiencing, but she averted her gaze for fear of what he might see in her eyes.

'Ah, yes . . . your letter.' There was a sneer in his voice when he rose to his feet and crossed the room to stand in front of the window with his broad, formidable back turned towards her. 'Your letter told me *everything,* and yet it told me *nothing*!'

Oh, God, how could he know that it was the most agonising letter I have ever had to write in my entire life! How could he know that I had written it with a total disregard for my own happiness, and with only *his* future in mind!

'Do we have to talk about something which happened five years ago, and which ought to be forgotten?' she asked, feeling wretched as she placed her empty cup on the table beside Nathan's, but she had injected an note of icy disapproval into her voice.

'Forgotten?' His voice was as harsh as his features when he spun round abruptly, and she flinched inwardly at the savage anger in his eyes. 'I assure you, my dear Julia, that I haven't forgotten a thing, and I don't ever intend to. I haven't forgotten how you led me on to believe that you loved me, and neither have I forgotten that cryptic little note you sent me because you were too cowardly to tell me to my face that you had changed your mind about marrying me. Do you know what I did with your engagement ring?' he demanded with that unfamiliar savagery that made her shirnk inside. 'I flushed it down the toilet. *Good riddance,* I said to *you*

as well as the *ring,* but meeting you again has made me realise that I can't put that episode in my life behind me until I know the reason for your deceit.'

Deceit! The word ricocheted agonisingly through her mind. She supposed that, one way or another, she had deserved his wrath, but he could not have hurt her more if he had launched a physical attack on her with a scalpel.

'I'm afraid that I don't have anything to add to what you already know,' she told him, rising abruptly with the intention of taking their empty cups through to the kitchen, but Nathan bridged the distance between them in a few long strides.

'Dammit, Julia!' he thundered at her, his fingers biting into her arm as he jerked her round to face him, and she paled at the look of intense fury on his ruggedly handsome features. 'I demand an explanation, and I'm not leaving here until I get one! I want to know what made you change your mind at the last minute, or had you planned your deceit from the start in order to derive some sort of macabre pleasure from the act of ditching me almost at the altar?'

Never, not even in her wildest dreams, had she imagined five years ago that her decision would have such savage repercussions, and she could not help wondering what she would have done at the time if she could have seen into the future.

'There is no truth in your hateful accusations,' she argued, trying desperately to remain calm in this moment of extreme distress. 'The reason why I broke off our engagement was that I realised in time that I didn't love you enough, and I knew that our marriage would be a mistake.'

'That's what you said in your letter, and I refuse to believe it *now* as much as I refused to believe it *then!*'

His eyes were like twin flames searing her, and she felt herself shrinking away from their probing intensity. '*Why,* Julia?' he demanded ominously, towering over her as the shadowy fingers of dusk reached into the room. 'What happened to make you change your mind about marrying me? Was it the thought that the chase would end for you with our marriage, and that you wanted to start the exciting ritual all over again with someone else?'

'Stop this ridiculous interrogation!' she pleaded, not sure how much more of this she could take before she cracked, and she was desperately afraid that she might reveal the truth. 'I didn't love you enough to marry you and go away with you, and there's nothing more to it than that!'

'You're *lying!*' he accused her harshly, taking her shoulders in a crushing grip. 'You're lying to me, Julia!'

For one fraction of a second Julia actually toyed with the idea of telling him what he wanted to know. She hated having to lie to him; she hated having to lie to *anyone;* but she feared Nathan's reaction to the truth. Would he despise her for what she had done, or would he feel obliged to her? She knew that she could cope with his condemnation, but she found the thought distasteful that he might feel under an obligation to her. And then there was Marcia. It was the thought of the woman he had been seeing for the past year that finally influenced her decision.

'I've told you the truth!' she persisted desperately with the abominable lies she had started five years ago.

'The *hell* you have!' he contradicted her savagely, jerking her taut body against his, and holding her a prisoner in the hard circle of his arms while his mouth descended on hers with a force that parted her lips.

Julia's hands were flat against his chest, the muscles

in her arms straining in an attempt to push him away,
and then, to her horror, all those long-buried emotions
stirred to life inside her. Her body yielded against his for
a fraction of a second before sanity prevailed, and she
pushed Nathan away from her with a burst of strength
she had not known she possessed.

She was trembling inwardly, and there was an angry
accusation in her grey eyes when she looked up at him
and croaked, 'You shouldn't have done that.'

'Perhaps not,' he agreed mockingly. 'But it has
shown me that you're not as indifferent as you'd like me
to believe.'

Julia spun away from him when she felt a rush of
embarrassing tears stinging her eyes, but she blinked
them away rapidly. She had had enough, she could not
tolerate much more of this, and she took a deep,
steadying breath before she said, 'Please leave,
Nathan.'

'I'll go, but you might as well accept the fact that you
haven't seen the last of me,' he told her with a harshness
that jarred her raw nerves and sent tremors of fear
racing through her body. 'I deserve an explanation, and
I refuse to settle for anything less then the truth.'

'Forget the past! It's over and done with, and there's
no sense in raking it up simply to bury it again!' She
stood with her back to him, not daring to face him until
she had managed to control her quivering features, and
she was praying silently that he would not prolong his
departure. 'Think about Marcia instead,' she added in a
voice which she hoped would sound persuasive. 'Your
future lies with her.'

She had put a knife to her own heart, but it was
Nathan who drove it in up to the hilt to draw blood. 'I
know where I stand with Marcia,' he said cuttingly,
'and I know I can depend on her to be there whenever I

need her.'

Julia started to shake like someone in post-operative shock, and her hands clenched spasmodically at her sides until her nails bit savagely into her palms.

'Goodbye, Nathan,' she said through her teeth, and she could not have made it any clearer that she wanted him to go.

'Not goodbye, Julia,' he contradicted her mockingly, coming up behind her and standing so close to her that she could almost feel the heat of his body against her back. 'We shall meet again, but until then I suggest you do some serious thinking. You owe me the truth, and I want nothing less from you.'

There was a threatening note in his voice, and it sent a shiver racing up her spine when he walked out of the cottage and closed the front door firmly behind him. Moments later she heard him drive away, and only then did she relax the rigid hold on herself to collapse on to the cane bench in a shuddering, sobbing heap.

The past and present had collided viciously to expose her as an emotional fraud. Oh, she had been so good at pretending to herself that she no longer cared, and she had actually begun to believe the things she had told herself, but that, too, had been a lie. She had never stopped caring, and it was futile to think that she ever would. Her love for Nathan had been too profound to be swept aside by time, and that was why his anger and his contempt had the power to cut so deep into her soul.

I know where I stand with Marcia, and I know I can depend on her to be there whenever I need her.

Dear God! Nathan could not have hurt her more even if he had tried, and the irony of it was that there was a great deal of truth in the words he had flung at her. She had not been there for him when he had needed her. She had been needed elsewhere, and she had turned her back on Nathan and his needs. She had done what she had considered was for the best, but that argument did nothing to raise her out of that deep pit of misery into which she had been plunged.

Julia did not stir until the dusk had turned to darkness outside, and her feet felt as if they had been weighed down with lead when she switched on the light in the kitchen and swallowed down two headache tablets with a glass of water. She was aching all over as if she had taken a physical beating, and her mind was whirling in total confusion. What had once seemed so *right* was now so terribly *wrong,* but she was not capable of seeking clarification for her crazy thoughts.

She opened the refrigerator and took out the piece of steak which she had wanted to grill for herself that evening, but she put it back into the refrigerator and slammed the door shut. If she ate something now she would be physically ill, and she decided instead to take a relaxing bath before she changed into something comfortable.

Her future suddenly looked as bleak as it had been five years ago. At that time she had still had the time-consuming task of nursing her grandmother through the various stages of the terminally ill, but now she had nothing . . . and no one!

Dammit! If she went on like this she would end up feeling sorry for herself, and that was the last thing she wanted to do.

Julia went to bed late that night, but she could not settle down and go to sleep. Her mind was replaying every agonising word that had been spoken between Nathan and herself earlier that evening, and she was still lying awake in the early hours of the Friday morning when she heard the wind-driven rain beating heavily against her bedroom window, but it came as no surprise to her. She had seen the rain clouds gathering over the distant hills during the previous afternoon, and she had lived in Doornfield long enough to know that this was not a shower which would be over in a few hours.

It rained all day Friday as if to match her dismal mood, and it was still raining the Monday of the following week when she went to work in the morning. The weather did not keep the patients away, and dripping raincoats and umbrellas left puddles of water on the tiled floor in the reception area. The waiting-room was packed when Roland arrived from his early morning rounds at the hospital, and it took almost three chaotic hours before the waiting-room started clearing.

It was during the course of that morning that Warren Chandler telephoned to invite Julia to dine with him at his restaurant in town. A refusal sprang to her lips, and then she thought, 'Why not?' She had not seen Warren for some weeks, and having dinner with him would be preferable to spending another evening alone at home with nothing but her miserable thoughts for company.

She accepted his invitation and, knowing that she was busy, he ended their brief conversation with an abrupt, 'I'll pick you up at seven.'

Julia did not question her decision to dine with Warren until she arrived home late that afternoon. She was tired and irritable, and she was not fit company for anyone, but she could not go back on her word.

It had stopped raining at last when Warren called at her cottage at seven that evening to collect her. Tall, lean and fair, he was immaculately dressed in a dark dinner-suit, and his dark glance was appreciative when she confronted him at the door in a blue chiffon evening dress which she had bought several years ago, but which refused to be dated because of its simple style.

'I like you in blue,' he complimented her. 'It adds

lustre to your eyes, and changes your skin to cool alabaster.'

His flattery always made her feel a little uneasy, but, for once, her morale needed a boost, and she smiled up at him with more warmth than she had intended when she locked her door and allowed him to escort her out to his Mercedes parked at her gate.

The Mopani restaurant was situated on the other side of town, and it had become a favourite gathering place among the locals since the first time Warren had opened its doors to the public two years ago. Diners had the choice of an indoor or outdoor meal. In good weather the mopani trees offered sufficient shade during the day, and at night they could dine beneath the coloured lights which trailed along the branches of the trees.

On this night the all-weather tables were deserted beneath the mopani trees. The diners had all chosen to eat indoors, and the restaurant was filled to capacity when Warren led Julia to his private table in a secluded corner at the far end of the restaurant with its attractive log-cabin décor.

This was not the first time Julia had dined with Warren in his restaurant and, as always, a bottle of vintage wine was brought to their table. The wine steward filled their glasses, left the bottle in an ice-bucket beside their table, and disappeared discreetly.

Warren raised his glass to Julia across the candle-lit table, and it was he who kept the conversation flowing while they drank their wine and studied the menu.

'May I recommend the *escargots* to start with this evening, and the *Poussin aux Aromates* to follow.'

Julia looked up from her menu to cast a dubious glance at Warren. 'I don't mind the baby chicken grilled with lemon and fresh thyme, but I'm not so sure about the snails.'

'The snails are sautéed with garlic in white wine, and simmered with cream and fresh parsley,' Warren explained. 'You'll enjoy it.'

'It sounds interesting,' Julia admitted, but she still had her reservations.

Warren placed their order and plied her with wine until their *escargots* were served. The wine had perhaps made her adventurous, she could not be sure, but she actually enjoyed her first taste of snails, and she relaxed to enjoy the rest of their meal.

'Dr Corbett came into the restaurant one evening last week to sample our cuisine,' Warren remarked some time later when they were drinking their coffee, and Julia's heart seemed to jerk uncomfortably in her breast at the topic he had chosen for conversation. 'I suppose you've heard that he's the fellow who bought Honeywell from Tant Sophie Breedt,' Warren elaborated on the subject, 'and I must say that the lady who accompanied the good doctor was quite a dish.'

'Mr Corbett is a specialist, and so doesn't use the title *Doctor,*' Julia explained, raising her cup to take a sip of strong, aromatic coffee, and congratulating herself on the fact that she could speak without a tremor in her voice.

'Do you know him?' Warren pounced unexpectedly.

'Yes,' she answered him abruptly, and she wondered if she was imagining that a certain tension had suddenly shifted into the atmosphere between them. 'I used to work in a Johannesburg hospital, remember?'

Warren's glance sharpened disquietingly on her face as he leaned towards her across the table. 'How well did you know him?'

'I knew him well enough to be able to tell you that he's a brilliant neuro-surgeon,' she answered him cautiously.

'You didn't know him privately, then?'

'Warren, what are all these questions leading up to?' she demanded with some annoyance.

'I'm not sure.' His dark glance held hers relentlessly. 'I saw an odd look in your eyes when I mentioned his name, and I'm trying to discover the reason behind it.'

'You're imagining things,' she admonished him, swallowing down a mouthful of hot coffee and trying desperately to quell that sense of alarm which was spiralling through her.

'Has anyone ever told you that you're a bad liar?'

'Has anyone ever told you that it's rude to pry into other people's lives?' she counter-questioned sharply.

'Then you *are* hiding something from me.'

'*No!*' That lean, handsome face across the table from her creased into a faintly triumphant smile, and her anger evaporated as she leaned back in her chair with a sigh of resignation. 'I really don't know why I should be telling you this, but Nathan Corbett and I were once engaged to be married.'

Warren's expression sobered as he continued to observe her closely. 'Who called it off? You, or him?'

'I did.' She lowered her gaze hastily to hide the pain of remembering. 'And please don't ask me to explain.'

Warren reached across the table to clasp her hand. 'Julia, I would like you to marry me.'

'If that was intended as a joke, then it's in poor taste,' she rebuked him.

'I'm not joking.'

No, he wasn't, she could see that now, and it flung her mind into confusion. 'But I don't—I mean you can't——'

'You don't have to give me an answer right away, and you don't have to be alarmed by what I have said,' he interrupted her, the pressure of his fingers increasing in a comforting gesture. 'I merely want you to know how I have felt since the first time I saw you, and if you ever need someone to lean on, I would like to think that you will come to me.'

In a matter of seconds Warren had altered their comfortable relationship into something which everything inside her felt compelled to reject, and it saddened her. 'I never guessed that you felt this way.'

'I'm a patient man,' he smiled, a teasing light in his eyes, 'and I have discovered that, when I'm patient, I nearly always get what I want.'

He pulled a comical face to ease the tension between them, and she laughed for what seemed like the first time in weeks. His intensity might have been unwanted before, but suddenly it was like a bracing tonic, and she relaxed completely while they finished their coffee.

It was ten o'clock before Warren took her home, and she was pleasantly tired when, ten minutes later, he turned into the lane that led to her cottage.

'It appears you have a late visitor.' Warren alerted her to the fact that a red Ferrari was parked at her gate, and her heart leapt into her throat at the sight of Nathan leaning against it with his arms crossed over his chest. 'Shall I stay, or would you prefer to see him alone?' Warren asked her when he had parked his Mercedes behind the Ferrari.

'I'd prefer to see him alone.' Was that choked, husky voice really hers? she wondered as she placed a detaining hand on Warren's arm. 'Thanks for a lovely evening, and please don't get out.'

'Shall I see you again?'

'Call me tomorrow,' she invited, leaning across impulsively to kiss his lean cheek before she got out of the car.

CHAPTER THREE

AN owl hooted in a tree close to the cottage when Warren drove away, and Julia shivered involuntarily as she stood watching the Mercedes' tail-lights disappear down the lane, leaving her alone with Nathan. Wisps of cloud drifted across the moon to bathe the earth in an eerie darkness, and the owl hooted once again as Julia turned to see Nathan push himself away from his car.

She could not see his face, but his tall frame was an ominous shadow moving towards her, and her hand fluttered nervously towards the gate to grip it firmly. 'What are you doing here at this time of night?'

'I was waiting for you,' he drawled with a ring of mockery in his deep voice. 'I thought it might be interesting to meet your latest conquest, but he left in such a hurry that I never caught a glimpse of the poor fool.'

Your latest conquest! Her throat tightened as if she had swallowed a piece of food which refused to go down.

'Go away, Nathan!' she hissed through her teeth, her fingers finding the latch on the gate as she spoke. 'Go away and leave me in peace!'

'The least you could do is invite me in for a cup of coffee,' he insisted, and in the darkness the familiar scent of his masculine cologne awakened memories she had tried so hard and so long to bury.

'It's late and I'm tired,' she protested with a desperate need to get away from him, and away from the feelings he seemed to evoke with such diabolical ease.

'I promise not to stay long.'

She heard that familiar note of determination in his voice, and a wave of helplessness surged through her. She knew from past experience that he was immovable once he had made up his mind about something, and nothing short of a bolt of lightning was going to stop him from accompanying her into the cottage.

It was Nathan's hand, not hers, that opened the gate and, taking her silence as acceptance, he ushered her along the stone path that led to her front door. She took her key out of her evening purse, but it was removed from her fingers to unlock the door and, switching on the passage light, Nathan stood aside for her to precede him into the cottage.

Julia did not look at him when she stepped inside and gestured towards the door on her right. 'If you would like to wait in the lounge, I'll——'

'The kitchen will do very nicely,' he interrupted her, and her jangled nerves coiled themselves into painful knots when he followed her down the short passage into the kitchen.

She switched on the light and left her evening purse on the table as she crossed the room to put water into the kettle. She heard the legs of a chair scraping on the tiled floor when he seated himself at the table, and her body tensed when she sensed that his razor-sharp eyes were following every movement she made. It angered her when she noticed the visible tremor in her hand as she plugged in the electric kettle and switched it on. *Damn* him! she cursed Nathan silently while she set out the cups and spooned instant coffee into each one. *Damn* him for making her feel like a specimen under a microscope!

'I always liked you best in blue,' he said, the scrape of

the chair legs on the floor jarring her sensitive nerves
when he got up and crossed the room to stand behind
her. 'There's only one thing wrong with your
appearance.'

'No!' she exclaimed in alarm, sensing his intentions,
but his hands were in her hair before she could stop him,
and the combs were deftly removed to let her honey-
brown hair cascade in glossy waves down on to her
shoulders.

'You have beautiful hair, Julia,' he murmured,
running his fingers through it. 'And it's still as soft and
as fragrant as I remember.'

She was too afraid to move when she felt him bury his
face in her hair. The heat of his body against her back
was suddenly a delicious torment, and she knew she had
to put a stop to it before her emotions got out of hand.

'Nathan, I think you should——'

'It's surprising how much I can remember about
you,' he went on as if she had not spoken, his strong
surgeon's hands in her hair making her scalp tingle.
'There's a little mole in the nape of your neck . . . yes,
here it is, and I can remember how you trembled when I
used to kiss it . . . like this.'

His mouth was like fire against the sensitive skin at
the nape of her neck, and her eyelids felt heavy when
those familiar tremors raced through her body to alert
every nerve and sinew to the pleasure of his touch, but
her mind shouted out a warning which she could not
ignore. If Nathan was out to rekindle old fires, then his
motive was revenge, and not love.

'Stop it, Nathan!' she cried out in fear and anger as
she twisted away from him into the corner of the wall
unit where the kettle was hissing as an indication that it
was heating the water. 'For God's sake, stop it!'

'Does your new boyfriend make you tremble when he

touches you?' Nathan demanded with a derisive mockery that made her cringe inwardly. 'Does the poor sap have any idea that your relationship will never progress because you are nothing but a tease?'

'A *tease?*' she echoed stupidly, too stunned for the moment to grasp what he was saying.

'Yes, Julia,' he smiled cynically, his black sweater and slacks heightening that element of danger lurking beneath his outwardly controlled appearance. 'You tease a man into believing that you want him as much as he wants you, but you will always back off just before he can got you into his bed.'

'Dear God!' she breathed, white to the lips and shivering inwardly as if the blood in her veins had turned to ice.

'I was the biggest sap of all,' Nathan laughed harshly, his blue eyes raking her contemptuously. 'I never pressured you too much because I was foolish enough to want to marry you before I took you to bed, and you played along until the very last before you backed out.'

Julia was shattered by the mental picture he had painted of her, and horror and revulsion fought for supremacy when she forced herself to meet his cold, contemptuous stare. 'Nathan, it—it wasn't like that at all!'

'How do you manage to look so innocently sincere while all the time you're a lying little *bitch*?' he demanded with a stinging disdain that was like a savage, crushing blow delivered directly to her heart. 'The water is boiling,' he changed the subject abruptly, glancing beyond her.

Only then did she hear the high-pitched whistle, and she turned sharply to switch off the kettle. Her hand shook violently when she tilted the kettle to pour water into one of the cups, and she somehow missed her mark, to pour water into one of the cups, and she somehow missed her mark, to pour boiling water over her hand which was resting on the cupboard beside the cup.

Her gasp of pain coincided with Nathan's exclamation of anger, and her hand was snatched and held beneath the cold-water tap. The flow of water eased the sting while Nathan took a tray of ice cubes out of the refrigerator and emptied them into the sink. He pushed the plug into the drain opening and Julia stood silent with agony as he lowered her hand into the swiftly rising water in the sink.

She bit down hard on her lip to stop herself from crying out in protest against the sting of the icy water against her tender skin, but she could not stop the tears that filled her eyes and spilled on to her pale cheeks.

Nathan was standing beside her, his hard chest against her shoulder and his breath fanning her cheek as he held her hand in the water. She wished that she could turn and rest her head against his shoulder, but she dared not, and she stared fixedly at that strong, slender-fingered hand grasping her wrist. Could he feel her pulse racing? Did he know what a sweet agony it was to be this close to him physically, and yet so far removed from him mentally?

'That was a damn foolish thing to do!' he spoke for the first time when the icy water had drawn the stinging pain out of her hand, and there was a reprimand in his voice that brought fresh tears to her eyes. 'Does it feel better?'

'Yes, thank you,' she murmured huskily.

'You fortunately didn't scald yourself too badly, but there might be a slight discomfort until the skin has healed properly.'

He lifted her hand out of the water, and she leaned against the sink, feeling exhausted suddenly when he

moved away from her to take a dry kitchen-cloth off the
rail against the wall. He stood facing her while he
dabbed at the moisture on her hand and studied the
pinkness of the skin against the back of her left hand.
His touch was gentle, almost a caress, and she could feel
the tremors starting all over again.

Nathan muttered something unintelligible when he
lifted his glance to look into her tear-filled eyes. He
flung the towel aside and, taking her quivering face
between his hands, he brushed his thumbs lightly across
her damp cheekbones. Their eyes met and held for
breathtaking seconds, and a little pulse was beating
rapidly at the base of her throat when he lowered his
gaze to her soft, trembling mouth. She knew he was
going to kiss her, but she felt powerless to do anything
about it, and his ruggedly handsome face became a blur
when he lowered his head to hers.

Her lips parted instinctively beneath the sensual
pressure of his mouth, and she welcomed this intimacy
she had spent five long years hungering for. Nathan was
kissing her with a lingering intent from which he
withdrew at length only to return his mouth to hers with
a new urgency which demanded a response she did not
have the power to withhold, and her hands slid from his
waist across his broad back to his shoulders as she
pressed herself closer to him. She was aware of his
arousal as much as she was aware of her own escalating
emotions when his arms crushed her slender softness
into the hard curve of his body, but the next instant she
was thrust aside with a roughness that made her stagger
back against the cupboard, and an icy coldness invaded
her heated body when she saw his face distorted with
fury.

'My God!' he exclaimed throatily and with a certain
amount of disgust while his disparaging glance raked

her from her honey-brown hair down to her small sandalled feet. 'I would never have thought it possible that I could still want you, but I do, and I *despise* myself for it!'

He turned on his heel and strode out of her cottage, slamming the front door behind him with a force that made the windows rattle in their frames, and a shuddering sigh passed Julia's throbbing lips when she stared dazedly at the cups she had set out on the cupboard. Nathan had not stayed to have his coffee, she thought foolishly, and then her vision blurred. Hot tears filled her eyes and trickled down past her nose until she could taste the salt of them in her mouth.

She did not hear Nathan drive away. She was crying too much to see or hear anything when she made her way to her bedroom, but his car was no longer parked at her gate when she drew aside the curtains some time later, and she cried herself to sleep that night for the first time in many months.

Julia did not hear her alarm go off the following morning, and it was the persistent ringing of the telephone in the lounge which finally managed to rouse her at seven o'clock. She leapt out of bed, snatching up her cotton robe and putting it on as she staggered barefoot from her bedroom into the lounge.

'Are you all right, Julia?' Warren's voice demanded when she had snatched up the receiver, and his anxiety was understandable when memories of the previous night came flodding back into her mind.

'Yes, I'm fine,' she assured him, subsiding weakly into the nearest chair and staring at the pink hue on her left hand which was still tender to the touch.

'Am I going to see you again?'

His uncertainty was touching, and it was perhaps unwise of her, but she saw in Warren the sanctuary she

she needed so desperately in this emotional storm which had erupted over her head.

'I'll see you whenever you wish, Warren,' she replied as she pushed her tousled hair out of her face, and she could almost hear him sighing with relief at the other end of the line.

'Perhaps some time over the weekend when it's not so busy here at the restaurant?' he suggested.

'I'd like that very much,' she agreed and, when they ended their conversation moments later, she rushed into the bathroom to shower and change into her uniform.

Julia skipped breakfast that morning, and spent the extra time with her make-up, but her attempts to disguise her puffy eyelids were not as successful as she had hoped. Roland took one look at her before he left the consulting-rooms to do his morning rounds at the hospital, and he muttered something about, 'So, we're back to that again, are we?'

She knew what he had meant. During her first lonely months in Doornfield she had cried herself to sleep many a night, coming to work with swollen eyelids the morning after, but Roland and Elizabeth had showered her with their friendship and understanding, and those tearful nights had finally dwindled into obscurity. She had thought that she would never shed a tear again, but . . . oh, God! . . . how foolish she had been to think that she would never have cause to cry again! All it needed was for Nathan to walk back into her life, and her calm little world was disrupted as if by a tornado. She had believed that her love for him was dead and buried, but she could not have been more mistaken. The pain was back, this time in multiple form, and a great deal more intense.

The weather was hot and humid after the rain, and

Julia's body felt clammy beneath her white uniform when she left the consulting-rooms to take her lunch-hour break on the Friday of that same week. She was contemplating having a long iced drink at a nearby tea-room when her attention was drawn to a silver Jaguar parked against the kerb. The man leaning against it was wearing a hat with a leopard-skin band, and the wide brim was pulled down over his forehead to leave his face partly in shadow, but there was something so familiar about him that Julia's steps faltered and slowed down.

'Could I perhaps give the lady a lift somewhere?' he offered, straightening to his full height, and that deep, gravelly voice was unmistakable.

'*Damian!*' Her face lit up with the sheer joy of encountering an old friend and, regardless of who might be watching, she flung her arms about his neck and kissed his leathery cheek. 'Oh, it's been such a long time!'

'Whose fault is that, may I ask?' he demanded, pushing his hat on to the back of his head and giving her a glimpse of that coppery hair she remembered so well.

'I plead guilty,' she smiled, raising her hands in a gesture of surrender, but her expression sobered the next instant. 'What are you doing here in Doornfield?'

'I was invited for the weekend, and I decided to stop in town to pay you a visit before I drive out to the farm.' Damian's green eyes were narrowed against the glare of the sun as he glanced about him. 'Is there somewhere in this God-forsaken place where one could get a decent lunch?'

'The Mopani restaurant,' she enlightened him, inwardly amused at this city man's description of the small village she loved so much. 'You must have driven right past it without noticing it.'

Damian opened the door on the passenger side of his

Jaguar. 'You'll have to direct me to it.'

'Is this an invitation to lunch?'

'It most certainly is, and I'm not taking "no" for an answer.'

Julia had no intention of declining his invitation, and Damian waited until she was seated comfortably before he closed the door and walked round to the driver's side.

'I've often wondered, Julia. Why Doornfield?' he asked her when he pulled away from the kerb and drove down the main street. 'I can understand your reason for wanting to get away from Johannesburg, but why didn't you go to Cape Town, or to Durban where you could have got a job in one of the hospitals?'

'After my grandmother died I needed the peace and tranquillity that Doornfield had to offer, and I've been happy here.' She did not add that she had been in such a dire state of physical collapse that she had been advised medically to take a complete break away from the city and the pressures she would encounter in a large hospital. 'The Mopani restaurnt is to your left up ahead,' she directed Damian when they approached a fork in the road.

'This is nice,' he smiled, the dappled sunlight setting fire to his hair as he glanced about him appreciatively when they had seated themselves at the only table which was still vacant beneath the shady mopani trees. '*Very* nice.'

Julia looked up to see Warren making his way towards them among the tables with their bright, checkered tablecloths.

'This is indeed a honour to have you here in the middle of the day, Julia.' He smiled down at her when he reached their table, but there was curiosity in the glance he cast in Damian's direction.

'Warren, I'd like you to meet an old friend from Johannesburg, Dr Damian Squires. Damian, this is Warren Chandler, the owner of the Mopani restaurant,' Julia introduced the two men.

'I'm delighted to meet you, Dr Squires.' The two men shook hands, and then Warren gestured towards the white-coated waiter hovering close to their table. 'Joseph will see to it that you have everything you desire, and I wish you both a pleasant lunch.'

Joseph stepped forward with the menus as Warren departed, and Julia and Damian both ordered an iced fruit drink to be served while they waited for their salad lunches.

'Pleasant-looking chap, this Warren Chandler,' Damian remarked when they were alone, and there was a smile about his wide, firm mouth which did not quite match the look in his green eyes. 'Has he become someone special?'

Julia shook her head and forced a smile to her lips. 'Warren is merely a friend.'

'It's still Nathan, isn't it?' Damian's astuteness should not have surprised her, but it did, and her startled glance merely confirmed his statement. That lazy, familiar smile curved his mouth as he leaned back in his chair with a hint of envy in his narrowed eyes. 'I hope I meet a woman some day whose love for me will be as unfaltering as yours for Nathan.'

'Nathan has Marcia now,' she reminded him stiffly, looking up to see Joseph walking towards their table with the iced drinks they had ordered.

'Marcia is a beautiful woman, but she's hard as nails and cold as ice.' Damian resumed their conversation when they were alone again, and his compelling glance held hers. 'Have you told Nathan why you broke off your engagement five years ago?'

'No, I haven't,' she confessed, taking a much-needed sip of her drink, 'and I don't ever intend to.'

'Why not?' he demanded with characteristic sternness.

'It won't do any good.'

'You can't be sure of that.'

Julia gestured dismissively with her hand. 'Please, let's change the subject, Damian.'

'I'm damned if I'm going to!' he persisted, his gravelly voice lowered and urgent as he leaned towards her across the table. 'You have got to tell Nathan the truth!'

'How do you think he will feel if I tell him that I broke off our engagement because I was afraid he might forfeit the chance of a lifetime to stay with me?' A look of distaste flashed across her sensitive features. 'The last thing I want is for Nathan to feel under an obligation to me.'

'*Sure* he might feel under an obligation, but if his love for you was sincere, and I have every reason to believe it was, then a sacrifice shouldn't be allowed to become a barrier between two people who love each other,' Damian reasoned with her. 'Loving someone isn't always the wine and roses people want you to believe. Too much wine could give you a headache, and roses have thorns. Making a sacrifice in the name of love is all part of that painful process of caring, but there *is* such a thing as having to endure too much pain.'

'Dr de Necker mentioned something similar a few weeks ago,' Julia heard herself confiding in Damian. 'He spoke about too long a sacrifice, and about shutting off my feelings so securely that one day I might find nothing left in my heart to give to someone else.'

Damian shook his head in disagreement. 'You haven't shut off your feelings. *Your* problem is that you have never *stopped* loving Nathan, and you've got to tell him the truth.'

'I can't!' Everything inside her shied away from the mere thought of it. 'If he's in love with Marcia then knowing the truth will serve no purpose . . . not for him, and certainly not for me.'

'It might make him human again, instead of the insufferable, unreasonable man he has become,' Damian argued the point, but Julia refrained from answering him when she saw Joseph approaching their table with their lunch.

Insufferable and unreasonable? Was that what Nathan had become? Julia wondered about this while they were eating their lunch. She had encountered an unfamiliar harshness in him, and a savage fury which she sensed needed very little encouragement to erupt. That did not necessarily mean that Nathan still cared for her. She had hurt his pride and his dignity, and he was merely giving vent to a long-suppressed anger which she understood and could accept despite the fact that it hurt.

'Nathan's having a *braai* out at the farm tomorrow evening,' Damian told her when they had finished their meal and sat with a second iced drink in front of them. 'Marcia will be there, and two other couples whom I haven't met yet, but this was such a last-minute invitation that I couldn't find anyone to invite along with me.'

Julia knew what was coming and she interrupted him hastily before he could ask the dreaded question. 'Don't ask me to be your partner for the evening, Damian, because I can't.'

Damian took his time about lighting a cigarette, but he did not take his eyes off her, and she was beginning to feel uncomfortable beneath his gaze when he asked,

'Do you want me to tell Nathan the truth?'

'*No!*' she gasped, almost choking on a mouthful of her drink.

'Then you will have to be there to keep me quiet,' he smiled at her triumphantly.

'That's blackmail!' she protested, her heart beating wildly against her ribs at the thought of what he expected of her.

Damian looked into her accusing eyes and shrugged carelessly. 'Call it what you will, but I'm serious.'

'I thought you were my friend.'

'I *am* your friend, Julia, but I'm also Nathan's friend, and I can't bear to see two people I care about destroying themselves like this.'

Her hand was shaking so much when she lifted her glass that she put it down again for fear of spilling. 'I can't tell Nathan the truth until I know what his feelings are for Marcia.'

'I will tell you what Nathan feels for her,' Damian growled fiercely, jetting smoke from his nostrils. 'She's beautiful, she boosts his ego, and she's available.'

'You shouldn't talk like that about the woman he might choose to marry,' Julia rebuked him even though she was driving a painful sword into her own heart.

'If he married Marcia Grant then he'd be a fool!' Damian exploded harshly.

'You can't really be sure of Nathan's feelings for Marcia, and neither can I.'

'How are you going to find the answer if you're so determined to stay out of his way?'

Julia felt as if she was being driven into a corner from which there was no escape, and her grey glance was pleading. 'Don't make life difficult for me, Damian.'

'My dear Julia, I'm not half as considerate as you are, and I shan't hesitate to tell Nathan the truth from *your* point of view as well as my own,' he continued relentlessly, a look of frustration and anger flashing across his face. 'My God, he needs to have some sense knocked into that clever head of his!'

'Damian . . .' She hesitated, her tortured mind spinning in its desperate search for a way out of this dilemma she was confronted with, but Damian was wielding a powerful weapon.

'Will you be my partner tomorrow evening, or do I drive out there now and spill the beans?' he demanded, and she knew him well enough to know that he would not hesitate to carry out his threat.

'I'll go with you,' she agreed, very much against her will.

'Good!' he nodded, crushing the remainder of his cigarette into the ashtray, and they finished their drinks in silence before he raised his hand to summon Joseph. 'May I have the bill, please?'

Joseph entered the restaurant and returned a few minutes later, without the bill. 'Mr Chandler said to tell you that he hopes you enjoyed your lunch, and there is no charge for Miss Julia and her doctor friend.'

Damian slanted an amused glance at Julia, and took out his wallet to give Joseph a substantial tip. 'You may tell Mr Chandler that I consider his hospitality overwhelming and very much appreciated.'

Joseph's face was split with a white-toothed grin as he bowed himself away, and moments later Damian was ushering Julia back to where he had parked his car.

'I guess there is another, more important reason why Warren Chandler has been so generous,' Damian remarked slyly when they drove away from the restaurant.

'Warren is just a friend,' she insisted.

'From your point of view perhaps, but not from his,'

he summed up the situation accurately, and a guilty flush stained her cheeks which did not escape Damian's notice. 'Yes, I think a little healthy competition might be just the thing Nathan needs at this moment to shock him out of this complacent world he is living in.'

She went cold and rigid with anxiety as she turned in her seat to face Damian, and her voice rose to a frantic pitch when she said, 'Damian, you're not going to do or say something which might give Nathan the impression that I——'

'Calm down, my dear,' he interrupted her in that soothing voice she had heard him use so often with his patients, and she drew a gulping breath to steady herself before she explained the reason for her anxiety.

'Nathan doesn't have a very good opinion of me at the moment, and dropping unfounded hints about Warren and me might substantiate Nathan's belief that I'm a—a *tease.*'

She almost choked on that hated word and looked away when she felt herself blush a furious red.

Damian's hand gripped hers briefly where it lay in her lap. 'I can promise you that Nathan won't say that again in my presence and get away with it.'

'Oh, Damian!' She sighed heavily and blinked away that film of unexpected tears. 'I know you merely want to help, but I wish you would leave well alone.'

Damian did not answer her, and during the short drive into town Julia hoped that he would free her from the ordeal of having to accompany him to the *braai* the following evening, but he obviously had no intention of doing so. He parked his Jaguar in the street outside Roland's consulting-rooms, and she knew it would be futile to plead with him when he asked for her address.

'I'll pick you up at five tomorrow afternoon,' he said when she had given him the necessary directions, and Julia watched him drive away moments later with a suffocating sensation gripping her chest.

CHAPTER FOUR

JULIA was not looking forward to the evening ahead of her, and her dread of having to go out to Honeywell had afforded her a sleepless night. She had prayed that something might occur to cancel the arrangement, but Damian had arrived at her cottage at five o'clock sharp on the Saturday afternoon, and he had been as adamant as the day before that she should accompany him . . . or else! She was not entirely convinced that he would carry out his threat, but she dared not take the chance. If Nathan had to be told the truth, then she would prefer that he heard it from her and from no one else.

She clasped her hands nervously in her lap, and her tension increased when Damian's silver Jaguar picked up speed on the open gravel road which led north to Honeywell. The soil was rich, and the climate was perfect for citrus and vegetable farming, but Honeywell had been a cattle-ranch known far and wide for its good-quality beef. Was Nathan planning to change all that? Her anxiety escalated at the mere thought of him, and her tightly clenched hands felt clammy.

'I presume Nathan is aware that you have asked me to be your partner for the evening?' She broke the silence between Damian and herself.

'I saw no reason to hide it from him,' Damian replied without taking his eyes off the road which lay shimmering ahead of them in the late afternoon sun.

Bitterness tainted the smile that curved Julia's soft mouth. 'I imagine he wasn't very pleased.'

'He didn't say a word, but I did happen to notice a brief look of dissatisfaction on Marcia Grant's face when I mentioned your name.'

There was a nervous flutter at the pit of her stomach when she glanced at Damian curiously. 'Do you think Marcia's aware of the fact that Nathan and I were once engaged to be married?'

'I have no idea what he's told her.' Damian frowned and turned his coppery head to meet her glance briefly. 'Marcia's a very possessive lady, and you might as well know that she considers every unattached female a threat to her relationship with Nathan.'

Julia's dread of the evening ahead of her was increasing with every passing second, and she changed the subject in the hope of easing the tension inside her. 'You mentioned two other couples.'

'The Marlows and the Sampsons,' Damian nodded, and a cynical smile curved his wide mouth. 'They're Marcia's friends rather than Nathan's, and I don't know much about them except that Marcia never surrounds herself with people who are not wealthy, or influential, or both.'

The words *wealthy* and *influential* made Julia lower her glance rather dubiously to her white cotton slacks and the sleeveless yellow knitted top. A *braai* was usually a casual, outdoor affair, but she was beginning to think that she should gave selected something more elaborate from her inexpensive wardrobe.

'You're not painting a very pretty picture of Marcia Grant,' she pointed out, glancing unobtrusively at Damian and finding a certain amount of comfort in the fact that he was wearing a white open-necked shirt, faded blue denims, and canvas shoes.

'I'm not trying to influence your opinion of her,' Damian assured her in a tight-lipped manner, 'but I think you ought to know what you're going to be up against.'

Julia felt like a junior nurse who was being primed by her superior before being sent to assist in the theatre for the first time, and a nervous laugh escaped her. 'Don't tell me you suspect that Marcia and I are heading towards some sort of clash.'

'The possibility cannot be overlooked.' Damian smiled at her briefly, but his smile never reached his green eyes beneath the straight, bushy brows. 'Marcia has a habit of dealing swiftly and viperously with someone whom she considers a competitor.'

'I have no desire to compete with her,' Julia protested with a measure of distaste.

'That isn't strictly true,' Damian contradicted her statement. 'If you were offered a second chance you would take it.'

He had a disconcerting way of digging down to the very root of a matter, but she was not going to let him startle her into making a confession.

'I'm not looking for a second chance,' she argued against that treacherous voice of her heart. 'When I ended my engagement to Nathan five years ago I knew that I would have to put that chapter of my life behind me for ever.'

'You may have put him out of your mind, Julia, but you have never put him out of your heart.'

She could not decide whether it was a liability or an asset to have a friend who knew her so well, but Damian had succeeded in stripping her of the will to persist with her denials, and her sarcastic reply was directed at herself. 'I'm sure Nathan has succeeded where I have failed.'

'It's a funny thing, Julia, but a man seldom forgets the woman he couldn't have.'

Don't do this to me, Damian! she wanted to cry out. *Don't give me hope where I know there is none!*

The entrance to Honeywell lay ahead of them, and Julia's heart was beating heavily against her ribs when Damian drove through the arched entrance and up between the grazing-camps towards the house which nestled amongst the tall, shady trees. She had visited the farm twice with Roland when it had still belonged to the Breedts, and she would never forget their warm hospitality, but she was not expecting the same reception from Nathan.

Damian parked his Jaguar beneath the half-dozen shallow steps leading up on to the wide veranda running along the south and east sides of the house, and she was relieved to see that the old-fashioned grandeur of the stone building had remained outwardly untouched except for the repair of the stone pillars which supported the thatched roof covering the veranda.

Julia slipped the strap of her white sling-bag over her shoulder when she got out of the car, and she was waiting for Damian to join her when something made her turn and look up to see Nathan framed in the entrance to the house. She was aware of a wild leaping of her pulses when he stepped out on to the veranda, and her senses were stirred at the sight of his tall, magnificently proportioned body in a brown shirt and creamy slacks which had been tailored to fit snugly across lean hips and muscular thighs.

'Hello, Nathan,' she greeted him with a calmness she had dredged up from somewhere, and she held out her hand to him when he came down the steps towards them, but his cool glance skipped over her, ignoring her gesture of friendliness as if she did not exist.

His snub sent a wave of heat into her face, but it receded the next instant to leave her chilled as she withdrew her outstretched hand self-consciously to clutch her white cotton jacket against her body in a subconscious attempt to add a little warmth to this icy, hostile world she had entered.

'That was quick,' he addressed Damian who had stepped up beside Julia to place an arm about her shoulders as if to comfort her in her moment of distress, and Nathan's eyes narrowed perceptibly as he followed the action.

'One of the things Julia could always be complimented on was her punctuality, remember?' Damian jogged Nathan's memory with a smooth deliberation which heightened Julia's discomfort.

Nathan's features tightened with anger, and Julia steeled herself for his response, but Marcia chose that moment to join them.

Elegant and sophisticated in a shimmering black top and close-fitting slacks, Marcia's speculative glance rested briefly on Julia before she linked her arm through Nathan's in a gesture which spoke clearly of possession. 'Darling, I think it's time to light the fire.'

Nathan nodded in agreement, and he once again addressed Damian as if Julia were not there. 'Come in and help yourself to a drink.'

Julia was reluctant to follow Nathan and Marcia into the house, and she leaned back hesitantly against Damian's protective arm.

'I would like to suggest that you forgive Nathan for his appalling lack of manners,' Damian remarked when Nathan and Marcia were out of earshot, and anger marred his usually amiable features.

'I shouldn't have allowed you to blackmail me into coming here this evening,' she replied in a voice which was calm despite the fact that she was shaking inwardly in the aftermath of Nathan's rude snub.

'It's obvious that Nathan intends to make you feel ill at ease, but you have the strength of character not to allow him that victory.'

Julia looked up into Damian's freckled face and forced her stiff lips into a smile. 'Thank you for trying to boost my morale.'

'Come, let me pour you a drink before I introduce you to everyone else.'

Damian ushered her into the house, and she was pleasantly surprised to see that the décor in the large entrance hall and living-room had been altered to project an image of lightness and airiness which appealed to her when she recalled how dark and dismal these rooms had once been. Sliding glass doors had been installed in the living-room, and it led out on to the side veranda where everyone had gathered in an area surrounding a newly built barbecue. A glass of wine was placed in Julia's hand, and Damian helped himself to a beer before he introduced her to the rest of Nathan's guests.

Jack Marlow and Walter Sampson were both businessmen from Johannesburg, and Julia guessed the ages of the two men and their wives somewhere between thirty-five and forty. The cut of their casual clothes indicated wealth, but both couples were so friendly and so totally unpretentious that Julia felt some of the tension easing out of her. Beatrice Sampson had been a nurse before her marriage, and discovering that she had something in common with Julia led to a lengthy conversation which helped Julia over those first awkward moments.

The fire had been lit, and the smell of woodsmoke permeated the air. The atmosphere was relaxing, but Julia could not shake off that awkward feeling that she was there on sufferance, and she was not blind to the fact that Marcia was observing her at times with a look of suspicion in her dark, almond-shaped eyes. Damian lingered at the barbecue with the men, but he did not neglect Julia, and he was quick to come to her rescue whenever he suspected that she might be feeling threatened.

The veranda and barbecue area were lit with coloured lights after sunset, and the meat was grilling on the glowing embers of the fire. The aroma was appetising, but Julia was beginning to suspect that she would not be able to eat a thing. Tension had gripped her throat during the course of the evening, and it was fast becoming an effort to speak. She had tried desperately not to glance in Nathan's direction, but her eyes had been drawn to him repeatedly as if by a magnet. She wished that she could have ignored him as he had ignored her all evening, but it was impossible. She was aware of him with every breath she took and every labouring beat of her heart. She was aware also of the easy intimacy between Nathan and Marcia. Every smile they exchanged was like a knife being given a vicious twist in her heart, and she could only pray that she was not making her emotional dilemma known to everyone else.

Julia had to admit that Marcia was a bright and charming hostess and, with the help of a servant, she brought out an array of salads which she arranged on the long table at the other end of the veranda. Everyone helped themselves when the meat was brought to the table, and Julia spooned food on to her plate which she knew she would have to make a pretence of eating. She helped herself to the smallest piece of *braaivleis* she could find, and when she looked up her glance collided unexpectedly with Nathan's. He held her glance effortlessly, and the icy indifference she glimpsed in his eyes struck deep. Her throat started to ache, and she looked away before he saw the tears which were stinging her eyelids.

Damian appeared at her side as if in answer to a call, and he involved her in a pleasantly casual conversation which gave her the opportunity to regain her composure without anyone noticing her predicament. Julia flashed him a grateful smile when they walked away from the table to sit down with their plates on their laps, and he winked at her encouragingly.

Music was relayed out on to the wide veranda from an indoor hi-fi system, and it was not long before the dancing started. Julia was not exactly in the mood to dance, but she could not refuse Damian, and they were dancing some distance away from the others when a hand on his shoulder made them stop abruptly and draw apart to find Nathan confronting them.

He was stony-faced, and there was something ominous in the rigid set of his square jaw when his cold glance flicked briefly in Julia's direction before settling on Damian.

'As one friend to another,' Nathan began in a voice that was cold and harsh, 'I think I ought to warn you that you're involving yourself with a woman who is totally without scruples. She is nothing but a tease who will play with your emotions and drop you flat for the fun of it.'

'Now, look here, Nathan! I think it's time you——'

'*Damian!*'

Julia had cried out his name instinctively, her hand gripping his arm to stop him in time, and her initial flush of embarrassment had faded to leave her pale when she realised that Damian was angry enough to reveal her secret.

'I'm damned if I'm going to let him insult you like

this!' Damian protested fiercely, his voice lowered to a harsh whisper to keep this verbal altercation private, but his green eyes were blazing with an angry fire, and his features had become set with a frightening determination.

'Damian, *please!*' she begged softly, her fingers digging urgently into the muscled flesh of his arm while terror was taking a suffocating grip on her lungs.

'She knows I've told you the truth,' Nathan cut in with a ring of savage cynicism in his voice. 'You'll make an idiot of yourself if you defend her, and that's what she's trying to prevent.'

Damian stiffened, and the warning pressure of Julia's fingers increased on his arm. She had never seen him this angry before, and she would not blame him if he revealed the truth about her, but . . . *please,* God, not now. Not like this!

'In all the years we've known each other,' he said at length, 'this is the first time I've had the desire to knock you down, Nathan, but it's not the strength of our friendship that has stayed my hand this evening, it's the knowledge that you will in time regret your vile accusations, and to have that on your conscience will be sufficient punishment.' Damian moved his shoulders as if to shake off his anger, and his arm relaxed at last beneath Julia's punishing grip as he turned to her and muttered, 'Let's go for a walk before I say more than I intend to.'

Julia did not protest when Damian ushered her away from Nathan and down the veranda steps into the moonlit garden. Fear had made her heart beat so hard and fast in her throat that it was some minutes before she could breathe normally again, and she walked with Damian in silence for what seemed like an eternity before she stopped and turned to face his shadowy form in the darkness.

'I want you to know that I appreciate your concern, but I would prefer you not to involve yourself with my problem, Damian,' she reasoned quietly. 'You were there five years ago when I needed someone to confide in, and I'm glad you know the truth, but the very last thing I want is to come between two people who have been close friends and colleagues for so many years.'

'Nathan has to be told the truth, Julia,' he insisted with that edge of fury still lingering in his voice. 'Your determination to remain silent is merely encouraging him to make these disgusting and degrading assumptions.'

'I'll tell him the truth,' she promised gravely, 'but I have to do so in my own good time.' The only answer she received was the sound of the music drifting out to where they stood in the shadows of the spacious garden, and she was overcome with mental exhaustion when she touched his arm imploringly. 'Do you think you could take me home?'

'Certainly,' he agreed roughly. 'I think I could do with a drive into town to cool off.'

'I'll have to get my handbag and my jacket.'

'I'll come with you.'

'That won't be necessary,' she declined his offer hastily. 'I'd prefer it if you waited for me in your car.'

'Perhaps that might be wise,' he laughed shortly. 'I'm still in the right mood to bash a few home truths into Nathan's head.'

'That's what I'm afraid of,' she admitted, leaving him there in the darkened garden to make her own way back to the house.

She did not see Nathan when she stepped on to the veranda to collect her handbag and jacket which she had left on her chair, and she had no intention of going in search of him merely to be snubbed and insulted once again.

'I hope we meet again some day,' Beatrice Sampson announced when Julia said a hasty goodnight to everyone, but Marcia had a look on her face that said, 'Not if I can help it!'

Julia took a short cut through the house to leave through the front door, but, to her dismay, Marcia followed her.

'I'd like a private word with you before you leave, Julia,' she said, opening a door into a room which had been changed into a small private lounge, and she stood aside for Julia to precede her into the room. Marcia's dark glance was coldly assessing when she closed the door behind her, and she came directly to the point. 'I know you were once engaged to Nathan, but that was in the past, and that's where Nathan and I would prefer it to stay.'

Julia had to suppress a crazy desire to laugh. Marcia had no way of knowing it, but she was flogging a battered and defenceless opponent, and Julia had her rigid training as a nurse to thank for the ability to mask her feelings behind an outwardly calm expression.

'I have no desire to rake up the past, and neither do I wish to rekindle an old relationship which is now as dead as ashes,' Julia answered her coldly, and at that moment she meant every word she said.

'I'm very glad to hear that, but I don't imagine it would do the slightest harm to warn you that I have no intention of tolerating your interference in our lives.' Marcia's crimson mouth was curved in a smile, but there was venom in the almond-shaped eyes that met Julia's unwavering glance. 'You had your chance with him once, but you lost it when you jilted him, and I know that he'll never forgive you for putting him through that humiliating experience. He's *mine* now, and you would do well to remember that!'

She was telling Julia nothing that she had not known already, but having someone like Marcia put it into words was like a heated blade being thrust into Julia's soul, and something deep down inside her forced her to retaliate.

'You're not very sure of Nathan, are you?'

'What do you mean?' Marcia snapped, her dark eyes narrowing with indignation and anger, but a tiny muscle jerked at the corner of her mouth, and it told Julia that she had struck a nerve. 'Of course I'm sure of Nathan!' Marcia insisted.

'No, you're not,' Julia contradicted her with a calmness which heightened Marcia's agitation to a level where the atmosphere in the room became explosive. 'There would have been no need to warn me off if you had been absolutely sure of Nathan's feelings for you,' Julia explained.

Marcia's breasts seemed to heave beneath the low-cut bodice of the black, shimmering top she wore with her slacks, and that spark of malevolence in her dark eyes was hastily concealed. Julia had an odd feeling that they were now circling each other mentally like two cats taking their time to sum up the opponent before launching into an attack, and it was Marcia who made the first move.

'What Nathan and I have together is something you will never be able to understand, or appreciate,' she smiled as if she knew that she was in complete control of herself and the situation. 'We meet each other's needs perfectly, and we're planning to make it a permanent partnership.'

Julia's heart lurched sickeningly in her breast. 'You're going to be married?'

Marcia's complacent smile was sufficient answer, and Julia could feel herself dying slowly inside.

'I can give Nathan what he wants, and much more. My father is an influential man, and he is in a position to ensure that Nathan's brilliance and skill as a neuro-surgeon will not go unnoticed.' There was undisguised malice in the smile Marcia bestowed on Julia. 'You wouldn't want to do anything which might rob Nathan of the chance to reach the top in his profession, would you?'

Julia felt sick and nauseatingly cold inside. It had been wrong of her to underestimate this woman. Marcia was shrewd, and fate had diabolically placed the most powerful weapon in her hands. No, Julia remonstrated with herself. I don't want to do anything which might rob Nathan of the chance to reach the top in his profession. If I did do something foolish, it would simply make a mockery of the sacrifice I made five years ago.

'No, you wouldn't want to do anything to hamper Nathan,' Marcia answered her own question with a triumphant smile while Julia continued to stare at her in abject silence. 'You're still in love with him, but you're never going to get him back. He belongs to me now, and that's the way he wants it.'

Julia knew that she would be physically ill if she had to stay in the same room with this woman a moment longer. She brushed past Marcia and, wrenching open the door, she rushed out of the house to draw the fresh air deep into her lungs in a desperate attempt to steady herself.

'Are you feeling all right?' Damian peered at her anxiously when she got into the car beside him. 'You looked a bit strange when I saw you rush out of the house.'

'I'm quite all right, Damian,' she assured him untruthfully. 'Just take me home, please.'

Damian did not need further encouragement. He turned the key in the ignition and drove away from the house with the Jaguar's headlights slicing through the darkness ahead of them.

This was a night which Julia would not forget in a hurry. Being ignored and insulted by Nathan seemed to take second place to the confrontation she had had with Marcia, and Marcia's words echoed relentlessly through Julia's mind until she thought she would go mad with despair. *We meet each other's needs perfectly, and we're planning to make it a permanent partnership. My father is an influential man, and he is in a position to ensure that Nathan's brilliance and skill as a neuro-surgeon will not go unnoticed. You're never going to get him back. He belongs to me now, and that's the way he wants it.*

It had not been in Nathan's nature to rely on the resources of others to get him where he had wanted to be, but five years was a long time, and his sense of values could have changed. He had been ambitious in his search for knowledge, but now it appeared as if he was ambitious in his search for the public recognition he could acquire in his profession. Could anyone change so drastically?

'Are you going to invite me in for a cup of coffee?' Damian intruded on her thoughts, and she came to her senses with the discovery that they were parked in her short driveway.

'Yes, of course,' she agreed hastily, getting out of the car and leading the way to the front door of the cottage where the outside light was sufficient for her to see what she was doing when she inserted her key in the lock.

'I owe you an apology.' Damian had followed her

into the kitchen and she turned to see him frowning down at the tiled floor. 'If I had known that Nathan would behave in such an atrocious manner, then I would never have insisted that you be my partner for the evening.'

'Don't feel bad about it,' she brushed aside his apology while she switched on the electric kettle. 'Nathan's behaviour was unpalatable, but quite understandable.'

'You're very forgiving.' He brushed the back of his fingers against her cheek while he studied her clincally. 'You're a little pale, and your skin feels cold to the touch. Are you sure you're feeling all right?'

'Yes, I'm fine,' she lied, turning from him to set out two cups, and they did not speak again until they were sitting at the table with a steaming cup of coffee in front of them. 'Do you know Marcia's father at all?' she questioned Damian cautiously.

'I don't know him personally, but I know *of* him.' His green glance was curious when it met hers across the wooden table. 'Why do you ask?'

'I'm curious, that's all.' She raised her cup and held it between her hands to force a little warmth into them. 'Is he a man of influence?'

'I would say so, yes. He had an interest in almost every conceivable venture, and I'm told that he has friends in all the right places.'

'Has he extended his interests into the field of medicine?' she continued to question Damian.

'It's odd that you should mention that,' he said, his brushy brows meeting in frown. 'Basil Grant is a major shareholder in a project which concerns the construction of a private hospital where wealthy patients may languish for a fat fee, and I've heard whispers that he is very keen to instal Nathan as head of the neuro-surgical department.'

Julia felt the cold hand of truth clutching at her heart. 'I imagine it's a chance in a lifetime.'

'That depends on which way you look at it.' His wide mouth twitched with the suggestion of a smile, but his rugged features were etched in disapproval. 'Nathan will most certainly make a name for himself, but at the same time he might also be selling his soul to the corporate bosses. He will be restricting himself to one particular hospital, whereas he now has the freedom to operate where he pleases, and you can bet that the members of the board will be selective when it comes to admitting patients.'

Julia could barely conceal her distaste, and she was having great difficulty in believing that the man she loved would allow himself to become a party to such unethical procedures.

'Has Nathan given you any indication as to whether he would accept such a post if it were offered to him?'

'Nathan doesn't talk much about himself these days. He works hard and plays hard, and he keeps his thoughts and feelings to himself.' His grave glance captured hers. 'He's not the same man you used to know, Julia.'

A lump rose in her throat and she swallowed it down with difficulty. 'Am I to blame, Damian?'

'Who can tell,' he shrugged. 'It knocked him hard when you broke off your engagement, but there are others who have survived similar knocks without undergoing major personality changes.'

Her empty cup went down into the saucer with a clatter, and she raised her hands to press her fingers against her throbbing temples. 'God knows, I've lain awake nights asking myself whether I made the right decision, but I've always seemed to come up with the same answer. I couldn't stand in the way of his career, and I knew that he wouldn't have gone to Europe without me.'

'You're quite right there,' Damian eased her mind slightly by confirming her statement. 'It wasn't an easy decision for you to make, and one day, perhaps, he'll appreciate what you did for him.'

She shook her head. 'I don't want Nathan's appreciation,' she whispered emphatically. 'I want him to be happy.'

Julia surprised herself with those words, but it was true. Nathan's happiness was more important to her than anything else, and if he could find that happiness with Marcia, then she would never dream of standing in his way. Her own feelings did not matter. She would survive as she had done before, but only if she knew that Nathan was happy in what he was doing.

'You're the only one who could make him happy.'

'No, Damian.' She tried to smile, but her lips quivered with the effort to suppress her tears, and resignation was mirrored on her pale face when she lowered her hands to meet his frowning glance. 'Nathan has changed, you said so yourself, and I can no longer give him what he wants.'

'I don't think he really knows *what* he wants, and taking extended leave at this time, and at this particular place, is perhaps one of the best decisions Nathan has made in a long time.' Their glances met and held for interminable seconds, then he smiled faintly and pushed back his chair to get to his feet. 'I could sit here all night talking to you, but it's getting late and, much as I dislike the idea, I have to get back to Honeywell.'

'Will I see you again before you return to

Johannesburg?' she asked when she rose to accompany him out to his car.

'I'm afraid not.' He shook his coppery head and smiled ruefully. 'I'm leaving early in the morning to keep a date with a pretty young girl before I take her into the theatre on Monday to do corrective surgery on a leg which she damaged rather badly in a car accident.'

'I'm glad you haven't changed, Damian.' She smiled up at him with a mixture of sadness and affection when they stepped out into the scented night air and walked along the concrete path to where he had parked his Jaguar. 'You're still the same caring man you used to be.'

He dismissed her remark with a careless wave of his hand, and glanced at her speculatively. 'Do you ever miss not working in a hospital?'

'Sometimes,' she confessed after a pausing to consider his query.

She had found it an exciting experience to be a part of the hospital team, but she was happy working for Roland de Necker, and he and Elizabeth had been good to her.

'Take heart, my dear,' Damian murmured, lowering his head to kiss her on the cheek. 'I'll keep in touch, and take care of yourself.'

Julia stood outside in the darkness for a long time after he had left, and only one clear thought emerged from her chaotic and tortured mind. Fate had brought Nathan and her together for a second time, but it was obvious now that they were not meant to have a future together. There would always be something which would create a barrier between them, and she had been foolish to allow herself to hope for more. There was no place for her in Nathan's life. He belonged to Marcia, they were going to be married, and his future would be secured.

CHAPTER FIVE

IT WAS peaceful strolling along the river at sunset with Warren. The picnic area was deserted, everyone had returned home after spending the Sunday along the shady banks of the river, and Julia inhaled the fresh country air deeply as if three years in Doornfield had not been long enough to rid her lungs of the city smog. A fish eagle swooped low over the rushing water, and they stopped to watch and listen to its familiar cry piercing the stillness that hovered over the bushveld at that time of day.

'The call of Africa,' Warren remarked when they resumed their leisurely walk.

'The cry of the fish eagle has been recorded often enough,' she agreed, raising her glance to see the sun dipping lower beyond the distant hills until it was out of sight. All that remained was a pink hue in the sky, and it awakened a sadness in her which she could not suppress when her thoughts drifted back to that afternoon two weeks ago when she had accompanied Damian to the *braai* at Honeywell. 'I never realised what I was missing when I lived in the city, and it's going to be extremely difficult for me to leave here,' she spoke her thoughts aloud.

Warren halted abruptly, and his fingers bit into her arm when he turned her to face him. 'You're not thinking of going away, are you, Julia?'

'It's something I might have to consider seriously at some time in the future,' she replied, knowing that she could not bear to stay in Doornfield once Nathan and Marcia were married. To see them together as husband and wife would be a form of torture which she had no intention of subjecting herself to.

'We've been seeing other more frequently these past two weeks.' Warren's dark glance held hers captive. 'Dare I believe that you're beginning to like me?'

'I have always liked you,' she answered him truthfully, 'but in the past I was always afraid that you might want more from me than friendship, and that's why I never encouraged you.'

'Are you encouraging me now?'

'I'm not sure,' she laughed self-consciously.

'Julia . . .'

'Take it slowly, Warren,' she pleaded hastily, her hands flat against his chest to ward him off when he would have drawn her into his arms. 'I like you, and I enjoy your company very much, but that's all I can say at the moment.'

'I'm not asking for much, Julia,' he said quietly, his hands moving against her shoulders in a caress which soothed rather than aroused her. 'I know you may never love me the way I love you, but I know I can make you happy if you would only let me try.'

A lump rose in her throat and her eyes filled with stinging tears. 'I think I'm going to cry,' she whispered shakily.

'Marry me, Julia.'

She shook her head and swallowed down that aching lump in her throat while she dashed away her tears with the back of her hand. 'I wouldn't be the right wife for you.'

'That's your opinion, not mine,' he persisted, his hands tightening on her shoulders.

'Warren, I . . .' Her protest died on her lips when,

for a brief moment, she actually found herself toying with the idea of marrying him, but she knew in her heart that it would be wrong, and her hands fluttered helplessly against his chest. 'I'm flattered and honoured, Warren, but I can't marry you.'

'Let me put it to you this way,' he said, obviously refusing to admit defeat. 'If you change your mind will you let me know?'

This was a reasonable request, and Julia considered it for a moment before she said, 'I can't promise anything, but, yes, I'll let you know if I change my mind.'

Warren kissed her briefly on the lips and, drawing her arm through his in the gathering dusk, she strolled back with him towards the path which led to her cottage.

Julia's thoughts were in a painful turmoil, and strewn with guilt. These past two weeks would have been sheer hell for her if it had not been for Warren, but it had been extremely selfish of her not to consider his feelings. He was in love with her and he wanted to marry her. She had known that for some weeks now, but she had done nothing to discourage him. Oh, God, how she hated herself at that moment!

'I believe young Tommy Durandt hurt himself rather badly a few days ago when he overturned a tractor on his father's farm.'

Warren's remark broke the silence between them, and it took a moment for Julia to surface from her disturbed thoughts. After three years in Doornfield she was no longer surprised or angered at the swiftness with which news travelled among the villagers.

'That young man should consider himself lucky to be alive.'

'How serious are his injuries?'

'Very serious.' A frown creased her smooth brow

when she recalled her own anxieties with regard to this young patient whom Roland had admitted to hospital three days ago with multiple injuries. 'I'm not really at liberty to discuss a patient.'

'I understand that Tommy Durandt had been chosen to play first-team rugby for his school before the accident,' Warren continued conversationally. 'Do you think his injuries will allow him to play again?'

'It's too soon to say,' she shrugged, giving him the only answer she could under the circumstances, and he fortunately left the matter there.

Warren had a cup of coffee with her at the cottage, and then he left. It was as if he had sensed that she wanted to be alone, and Julia was grateful to him for that. He was perceptive to her needs, and that was one of the many things she liked about him. Warren Chandler was a good, hard-working man, and he would make some woman a wonderful husband, but she could not imagine herself as his wife. She loved him in a way, but not as a woman ought to love the man she married, and Warren deserved better than that.

Nathan. Oh, if only she could shut him out of her mind and her heart! He was everything she had always wanted in a man, but fate had decreed that he would never be hers. Dear God, why did she still have to love him so much?

For some obscure reason Roland's waiting-room was always crowded on a Monday morning, but Julia did not object to being kept busy. It took her mind off her own problems, and she was pleasantly tired during a welcome break that afternoon when she prepared a tray of tea and took it through to Roland in his consulting-room.

He was sitting with his back to her while she poured their tea, and he was drumming his fingers on the arms of his chair while he studied a set of X-rays on the scanner.

'Tommy Durandt?' she guessed intuitively.

'Yes,' he grunted, snapping off the light on the scanner and frowning heavily when he removed the X-rays and slipped them into a large brown envelope on his desk. 'I'm worried about him, Julia.'

'Isn't he responding to treatment?' she asked, passing him a cup of tea.

'His condition has stabilised, and most of his injuries will heal, but the spinal contusion is causing complications.'

'His legs?'

'Non-functional.' Roland confirmed what Julia had begun to suspect. 'I've ordered a second set of X-rays which should be ready later this afternoon, and I'm placing young Tommy in the hands of a specialist.'

She nodded in agreement, and lowered herself into a chair to take the weight off her aching feet. 'Are you going to have him transferred to Pietersburg?' she asked, taking a sip of her hot tea.

Roland observed her speculatively over the rim of his cup and shook his greying head. 'Why risk having the patient transferred when we have an eminent specialist languishing in our own district?'

Julia's heart skipped a nervous beat, and her hands were trembling to the extent that she almost spilled her tea. 'You can't possibly be referring to Nathan?'

'I am,' Roland nodded, capturing her startled glance. 'He'll be here at five this afternoon to take a look at the X-rays before we go to the hospital.'

'You mean he agreed?' she asked stupidly.

'Without hesitation.' Roland observed her closely from behind his gold-rimmed spectacles. 'Did you expect him to refuse?'

'I . . . no . . . I wasn't sure,' she faltered helplessly.

'I'm convinced that if anyone can help Tommy Durandt, then it will be Nathan Corbett.' Roland drank his tea quickly and he was smiling faintly when he leaned across his desk to place his empty cup on the tray. 'Perhaps I should explain that Nathan has featured quite frequently in the medical journals during these past two years, and he has built up quite a reputation for himself as a miracle-worker.'

This did not surprise her. She had always known that Nathan was destined for great heights in his profession, and now she knew that he had succeeded.

'You won't need me here after five this afternoon, will you? she asked with a desperate need to be out of the way before Nathan arrived, but Roland swiftly dashed her hopes.

'I would appreciate it if you would stay long enough to make us a cup of coffee when Nathan arrives.'

'Very well,' she agreed dully, discarding the cup of tea she had barely touched, and taking the tray with her when she rose to her feet.

'Julia.' He stopped her before she could reach the door, and she glanced at him over her shoulder. 'Young Tommy deserves the best.'

'Yes, of course he does,' she agreed without hesitation, but she was shaking inwardly when she closed the consulting-room door behind her and carried the tray into the small kitchen.

Julia was not sure how she had managed to get through the remainder of that afternoon without a serious mishap occurring. Her thoughts had been centred on Nathan, and her nervousness had increased as the afternoon progressed. She dreaded having to face him again after she had been forced to endure his rudeness and his insults at their last meeting.

Her palms felt clammy, and her insides were coiled into tight, painful knots when the hands of the electric clock on the wall shifted closer to five o'clock. She prayed that Nathan would be late, or that Roland would change his mind about wanting her to stay, but the minute hand of the clock had barely shifted on to the twelve when Nathan walked into the waiting-room.

A pulse was beating erratically at the base of her throat, and the fan on the filing-cabinet seemed to be whirring loudly enough to make her head ache. Her subconscious mind registered the proud, arrogant tilt of his dark head, and the width of his shoulders beneath the beige, lightweight jacket. His white shirt was unbuttoned at the throat, giving her a tantalising glimpse of the dark hair curling against his tanned chest, but she pulled herself together sharply when she raised her eyes to encounter his cool blue gaze.

'Dr de Necker is expecting you,' she said stiffly, her legs shaking uncontrollably beneath her when she stepped out behind her desk. 'If you'll come this way, please.'

'I have called at your cottage several times these past two weeks,' he said, barring her way with a few long strides. 'Were you out, or were you pretending not to be home?'

Her nerves jolted in surprise and resentment, but she somehow succeeded in remaining outwardly cool and calm. 'I can't imagine why you wanted to see me, and neither can I think of anything we might have had to say to each other.'

'I can think of quite a few things we have to say to each other, but it will have to keep for the moment.' His smile was mocking when he stepped aside to let her pass. 'Lead on.'

Julia knocked on Roland's door and opened it without waiting for a reply. 'Mr Corbett is here to see you, Dr de Necker.'

'Ah, yes.' Roland smiled and rose from his chair to walk round his desk when Julia stood aside for Nathan to enter. 'I'm very glad to meet you at last, Mr Corbett.'

Julia slipped out while the two men shook hands, and she was shaking so badly that she had difficulty in making the coffee which Roland had requested earlier that afternoon.

Damn Nathan for having the ability to make her feel on edge and unsure of herself! If only she could acquire some of that icy indifference he displayed towards her. Oh, God, if only she did not have to care so much!

Roland and Nathan were studying the new set of X-rays on the scanner when Julia entered the consulting-room with their coffee, and they were discussing their findings in lowered voices when she placed the tray on Roland's desk. They appeared to be oblivious of her presence, and she was retreating quietly when Roland said, 'Thank you, Julia. You may go home now.'

Nathan's head snapped round, and his narrowed gaze collided with hers. There was something intensely disturbing in his piercing appraisal of her, and she murmured a hasty 'goodnight' as she left the consulting-room, collected her things, and went home.

Warren had invited Julia to have dinner with him that evening. He was a marvellous conversationalist, but her mind wandered constantly, and she had difficulty in concentrating on what he was saying.

What had Nathan decided? Would he operate on Tommy Durandt, or had he discovered that there was nothing worth while he could do for the young man? Why had he looked at her so strangely when she had taken the coffee into the consulting-room? How was she supposed to interpret that disturbing expression in his eyes, and . . . *dammit* . . . why did she have this uneasy feeling about it?

'I'm glad you were free to have dinner with me this evening.' Warren succeeded in capturing her wayward thoughts while he and Julia were eating their dessert. 'My sister is going to be married next week Saturday, and my mother has asked me to help with the arrangements.'

'When do you have to leave?'

'I'm motoring down to Durban in the morning.' His hand reached for hers across the table, and the flame of the candle between them danced in his dark, smiling eyes. 'Will you miss me while I'm gone?'

'I imagine I shall,' she admitted, smiling back at him, and his fingers tightened about hers.

'I wish you could come with me. I know my mother would adore you.'

Julia's thoughts took an irrevocable swing towards Nathan. His parents had died long before she had met him, but he had a married sister living in Zimbabwe with whom he had corresponded regularly.

'Excuse me, sir,' Joseph intruded apologetically. 'There is a telephone call for Sister Henderson.'

Julia looked up with a start, and a coldness filtered into her veins. Who would have taken the trouble to seek her out at the Mopani restaurant . . . and why?

'Sister Henderson will take the call in my office,' Warren was saying, rising to his feet with Julia.

'Yes, sir,' Joseph nodded, leaving hastily to have the call transferred to Warren's office.

'This way, Julia.' Warren's expression was curious, but he did not question her when he took her arm to usher her across the restaurant and into a small, private office. He gestured towards the telephone on his desk, and smiled into her apologetic eyes as he turned towards the door. 'I'll wait for you at our table.'

She murmured her thanks and waited until he had closed the door behind him before she lifted the receiver. 'Julia Henderson speaking.'

'Forgive me for intruding on your dinner engagement, Julia, but I need to speak to you rather urgently.'

Her heart lurched anxiously in her breast at the sound of Roland's voice. 'What's wrong?' she croaked nervously. 'What has happened?'

'This isn't something I want to discuss on the telephone,' Roland answered her abruptly. 'If Warren wouldn't mind dropping you off here at my place, then I'll see to it that you get home safely.'

'I'll be there as quick as I can,' she said, seeking refuge behind a professional attitude, but her hand was trembling when she replaced the receiver on its cradle.

'What's the matter?' Warren questioned her gravely when she arrived at their table to collect her wrap and her evening purse.

'I don't know,' she answered him truthfully. 'Dr de Necker wants to discuss something with me at his home. He says it's urgent, and that he'll see me home later.'

'I'll take you at once,' Warren offered without hesitation.

'I'm sorry our evening has been cut short,' she apologised when they were driving away from the restaurant in his Mercedes, and his hand found hers briefly in the darkness.

'There will be other evenings.'

Julia did not answer him. She was too perturbed about this summons from Roland. She wondered briefly if this had something to do with Tommy Durandt, but she could not imagine what Roland would want to discuss with her which was of such extreme urgency that she had to be called away from her dinner-date with

Warren.

'Don't get out,' she said, her hand reaching for the door catch when he had parked his car in the street outside the de Necker home. 'Thanks for a perfect meal, and I wish you a safe trip in the morning.'

'I'll call you from Durban.'

'I'd like that,' she smiled, accepting his kiss on her cheek before she got out of the car and closed the door.

Warren waited until she had pushed open the wrought-iron gate and was walking up the curved concrete path towards the front door of the house before he drove away, but Julia was only vaguely aware of his departure. Her heart was beating heavily against her ribs when she walked quickly up the steps on to the well lit porch with its potted ferns, and she despised herself for the tremor she noticed in her hand when she rang the doorbell.

The door opened a few seconds later and Elizabeth smiled welcomingly as she drew Julia inside. 'Roland is waiting for you in his study, and he said I was to send you in the moment you arrived.'

Julia knew her way about the house, and she nodded without speaking. Her mouth felt as dry as dust when she crossed the carpeted entrance hall at a brisk pace, and her uneasiness had intensified until it felt as if her insides had been clamped in a vice. She paused in the dimly lit passage to wipe her clammy hands on the wide skirt of her peach-coloured evening dress, and she braced herself mentally before she tapped lightly on the study's panelled door and opened it.

Roland was seated on the corner of his desk, but Julia's nervous glance was drawn as if by a magnet towards the man who was rising from one of the leather armchairs, and for one terrible moment she was tempted to turn and run.

'Thank you for coming so promptly, Julia,' Roland was saying, and Julia dragged her eyes away from the odd intensity of Nathan's penetrating glance to see Roland waving her towards a vacant armchair.

'You said it was urgent.' There was a nervous catch in her voice, and she sat down quickly before her trembling legs decided to cave in beneath her.

'And so it is.' Roland gestured towards the fresh tray of coffee on his desk. 'Would you like a cup?'

'No, thank you.' Out of the corner of her eye she could see Nathan lowering himself into the armchair he had vacated on her arrival, but she did not shift her gaze from Roland. 'Does this have something to do with Tommy Durandt?' she asked bluntly.

'Yes, it does,' Roland confirmed her suspicions. 'Shall I tell her, Nathan, or will you?'

'I'll tell her.'

Tell me what? she demanded frantically as Nathan rose from his chair, and she had no option but to look at him when he followed Roland's example and seated himself on the corner of the desk nearest to her.

'There is a slight chance that Tommy Durandt might walk again, but it will require a major operation which I have agreed to perform. The theatre is available at five o'clock tomorrow afternoon, and I want you there to assist me with the operation.'

'You can't be serious!' Julia's incredulous glance darted to Roland and back to Nathan as a terrible suspicion manifested itself in her mind. 'If you have agreed to operate on condition that I will assist you in the theatre, then I think it's despicable of you!'

'It's not a condition, it's a request,' Nathan corrected her tersely, and there was anger in the cool blue glance that held hers.

'I doubt that the matron will grant you request when

there are fully qualified theatre sisters at the hospital who would assist you admirably,' she tried to reason with him.

'It has all been arranged with the hospital superintendent, and matron has agreed to it.'

'I don't suppose she was left with a choice, and you had no right to arrange something like this without first consulting me,' Julia protested, trying to control her rising anger.

'I'm asking you now.' Nathan's challenging glance held hers relentlessly. 'Will you assist me?'

The atmosphere in the study was tense and strained, and Julia had the most frightening feeling that the walls were closing in on her to restrict her breathing. She got up jerkily, and the skirt of her silk dress rustled in the silence as she walked towards the open window to draw the cool night air into her tortured lungs.

'The last time I worked in a theatre was five years ago.' She turned to face the two men in the room, and shook her head. 'I'm sorry, but I couldn't possibly agree to this.'

'I need someone in the theatre with me who is familiar with the way I work.' Nathan rose from the desk to walk towards her, and it seemed as if, mentally and physically, she was being driven into a corner. 'This is a very dangerous and delicate operation, Julia, and a fumbling theatre sister is something I shan't tolerate.'

'What makes you think that I shan't fumble?' she demanded, nervous anxiety making her voice rise a pitch higher. 'For God's sake, Nathan, I'm as rusty as hell!'

His mouth twitched with the suggestion of a smile. 'I don't believe you are.'

'Roland?' Julia shot a pleading glance at her employer, but she received no assistance from him.

'Elizabeth has agreed to help out in the consulting-rooms tomorrow afternoon,' he enlightened her calmly.

Julia felt trapped, and she disliked the feeling intensely. Why was Nathan doing this to her? *Why?* Was this yet another way in which he could hurt and humiliate her?

She passed a shaky hand over her eyes before she raised them to meet Nathan's challenging glance. 'It seems as if I'm left with no choice but to agree.'

His sensuous mouth curved in a triumphant smile. 'Thank you, Julia.'

'Don't thank me *yet!*' she snapped, striding towards the desk to escape his disturbing nearness. 'I think I could do with that cup of coffee I refused earlier.'

There was a hint of an apology in Roland's weary eyes when their glances met, but Julia was not in a forgiving mood. She was happy for the patient's sake that it was Nathan who would perform the operation, but she was petrified at the thought that she would have to assist Nathan in the theatre. *Damn him for doing this to her!* Five years was a long time, and she was not at all sure that she would cope. Her hand was trembling when she poured herself a cup of coffee, and she gulped it down black and without sugar. It did not steady her nerves, but it hit her stomach in the right place with a comforting warmth when everything else inside her felt as cold as ice.

'I'll give you a lift home,' Nathan offered, putting on his jacket, and she hesitated nervously before she collected her wrap and her purse and said goodnight to Roland.

Julia did not see Elizabeth before she left the house, but it was perhaps just as well. She was not in a fit state to have a normal conversation with anyone, and she was also too infuriated to appreciate the luxurious interior of Nathan's Ferrari.

The drive to her cottage took less than ten minutes, but Julia maintained a stony silence despite Nathan's vague attempts at making conversation, and she was leaping out of the car the moment he parked it outside her cottage.

'Thanks for the lift,' she said, slamming the door behind her with unnecessary vigor, but Nathan caught up to her before she could undo the catch on the garden gate.

'I'm coming in with you,' he said, taking her arm in a firm grip and propelling her along the path to the front door.

'No, you are *not* coming in with me!'

'You can't stop me.'

Her purse was taken from her before she could do anything to prevent it, and she was shaking with helpless rage while Nathan snapped open the fragile catch to search for her key.

'How dare you!' she cried, clenching her hands at her sides to suppress the desire to strike him.

'Stop this melodrama!' he ordered sharply, unlocking the door and switching on the passage light before he took her arm once again to propel her inside. 'All I want to do is talk to you, and there is absolutely no reason for you to behave like a petrified virgin in fear of being raped.'

A slap in the face could not have been more sobering, and she calmed down considerably. 'I'm tired, Nathan, and it's late.'

'It's ten thirty,' he said abruptly, glancing at the gold watch strapped to his lean wrist. 'I doubt that you would have complained had Warren Chandler kept you out this late.'

She stiffened at that hint of mockery in his voice. 'I

happen to enjoy Warren's company.'

'Meaning you don't enjoy mine?'

'Correct!' she snapped, walking into the lounge and switching on the reading-lamp beside her favourite armchair.

'I owe you an apology, Julia,' he said unexpectedly, following her into the lounge. 'My behaviour was inexcusably rude the other evening when Damian brought you to Honeywell, and Damian was right about one thing . . . I do regret it.'

She closed her eyes to halt the sudden rush of tears. His apology had stripped her of her defensive anger, and the tension was easing out of her body to leave her infinitely tired.

'Forget it,' she said, not trusting her voice above a whisper, and his hands were warm against her shoulders when he turned her to face him, but she dared not look at him.

'Does this mean that I'm forgiven?'

'Yes, you're forgiven.'

'*Dammit,* don't *do* that!' he exploded with a harshness that made her flinch visibly, and she bit down hard on her lip when his hands tightened on her shoulders in a punishing grip.

'Don't do *what?*' she gasped confusedly, looking up at last to encounter an unfathomable anger in those blue eyes blazing down into hers.

'Don't always be so damned forgiving!'

'All right, I *won't* forgive you!' she retorted furiously placing her hands flat against his hard chest and pushing him away from her. 'You were rude and insulting, and you don't deserve to be forgiven!'

'That's better,' he smiled twistedly, but that spurt of anger had left her drained, and she did not resist when he led her towards the cane bench and drew her down beside him. 'Why did you pretend that you wanted to marry me when you must have known that you had no intention of allowing our relationship to progress that far?'

Julia was instantly on her guard, and she shrank from him into the corner of the bench. She sensed a trap in his erratic and confusing behaviour, and she would walk right into it if she was not careful.

'Isn't it about time you went home to Marcia?' she counter-questioned coldly.

'Marcia doesn't live with me.' There was a stabbing mockery in the eyes that met hers. 'She's head of a thriving cosmetic company in Johannesburg, and it keeps her pretty busy.'

'When you told me that you were involved with Marcia I naturally assumed that she would be staying with you at Honeywell,' she explained, wishing she had kept her mouth shut.

'You assumed incorrectly.' He shifted his arm along the back of the bench behind her shoulders as he leaned towards her, and his knee brushed disturbingly against her thigh. 'I don't want to talk about Marcia, I want to talk about *us.*'

'I don't want to discuss the past, Nathan.' She looked away and shifted her position slightly to avoid that disturbing contact with his body. 'It's over, and I want it to stay that way.'

'It won't be over until I have satisfied myself as to the reason why you changed your mind about marrying me, but we'll leave it there for the moment.' His fingers were beneath her chin, tipping her face up to his and forcing her to look up into his probing eyes. 'How do you feel about tomorrow?'

'I'm scared,' she heard herself confessing while every nerve in her body had become centred on those strong fingers stroking the curve of her jaw.

'So am I.'

Her eyes widened in disbelief. 'You're just saying that to make me feel better.'

'It's going to be an extremely tricky operation,' he warned with an unexpected mixture of humour and gravity. 'That's why I want you there with me. We worked well together on those occasions when you assisted me as theatre sister, and I'm going to need all the luck I can get.'

'You don't need to rely on luck,' she rebuked him quietly. 'You're a skilled surgeon, and you were always at your best when the odds were at their longest.'

Nostalgic memories of the past blended with the present, and when she looked into his eyes she could feel herself melting with that familiar need which had been growing instead of diminishing over the years. Her heart was thudding in a wild tattoo against her ribs when his hand slid beneath her hair to seek out the sensitive nape of her neck, and his face became a blur when she felt his warm breath against her mouth. He was going to kiss her and, God knew, she wanted him to, but sanity returned with the sobering knowledge that she would be trespassing on Marcia Grant's property.

She drew a jerky breath, and turned her head away a fraction of a second before his lips touched hers. 'You really must go, Nathan. Please . . . I'm tired and I—I'd like to go to bed.'

She was feeling sick with misery and unassuaged longing when he drew her to her feet with him. She wanted desperately to feel the strength of his arms about her, but she dared not even contemplate it.

'I'll see you tomorrow,' he said, tilting her face up to his when she would have preferred to avoid meeting his eyes. 'I'd like you at the hospital an hour before the time.'

'I'll be there,' she promised, her heartbeats subsiding and her feelings carefully concealed behind her outwardly calm exterior, but she wondered if she would sleep at all that night while knowing what lay ahead of her the following afternoon.

'Four o'clock, and don't be late,' he warned sternly.

Julia was still standing where he had left her when she heard him drive away, and she was alone with her thoughts and fears and that terrible emptiness which only Nathan could fill.

'Dear God!' she groaned. 'I have got to stop loving and wanting him!'

CHAPTER SIX

THE operating-theatre at the Doornfield hospital was modern and well equipped, and Julia had donned a sterilised theatre gown and cap to conduct a final check with the theatre staff to ensure that everything would be as Nathan wanted it. She was not as rusty as she had imagined, and she was amazed at the ease with which she slipped back into the role of theatre sister. It was as if she had never relinquished that task.

She had arrived at the hospital punctually at four o'clock that Tuesday afternoon to find Nathan waiting there for her. He had instructed her briefly but methodically as to the intricate nature of the operation he was to perform, and now, as the minute hand on the large theatre clock moved inexorably towards five o'clock, Julia experienced that familiar tension which she had always encountered before an operation.

The patient had been wheeled in and transferred to the operating-table, the anaesthetist was prepared and waiting, and Julia was casting a final, critical glance at the instrument tray when the doors were pushed open and Nathan walked in.

'Here's Mr Corbett now,' the young theatre nurse whispered unnecessarily and with obvious reverence as they watched Nathan approach the operating-table with those long, loose-limbed strides Julia knew so well.

The past and present seemed to come together with a

shattering force while Julia stood looking at Nathan's tall, wide-shouldered frame in the green theatre garb and, if someone had asked, she would have had difficulty trying to explain her feelings at that moment. Pride? Respect? Awe? She was experiencing all three of those emotions, and several more, when she stepped forward, as she had always done in the past, to help him fasten the tapes of his mask. He turned at length to face her, his eyes a startling blue above the white mask, and the last fragment of her nervousness seemed to disintegrate beneath his calm, reassuring glance.

'Are you ready?'

The deep timbre of his voice fell pleasantly on her ears, and her grey eyes smiled up at him over her theatre mask. 'I'm ready.'

Nathan nodded to the anaesthetist, and a few seconds later he held out his gloved hand with an abrupt, 'Scalpel.'

Julia slapped the instrument into his palm, her confidence in her capabilities restored, and for the next three and a half hours nothing else seemed to exist beyond the operation which was in progress beneath those bright theatre lights. She watched in fascination, marvelling at the extent of Nathan's skill, and the steadiness of his strong, slender-fingered hands, while he worked on the severely damaged nerve tissues. She had seen him operate many times before, and she had always been aware of his brilliance as a neuro-surgeon, but on this occasion she knew that she was observing a polished professional. 'A miracle-worker', Roland had called him, and that was exactly what she was witnessing. Nathan was performing a miracle on this young patient's spinal column, and she had no doubt at all that the fair-haired Tommy Durandt would walk again.

She could barely conceal the glow of admiration in her eyes when the patient was finally wheeled out of the theatre, and she could not blame Nathan for the look of satisfaction on his face when he pulled down his mask and stripped off his rubber gloves.

'Thank you, Julia,' he said, smiling at her when they had changed out of their theatre gowns and were drinking a cup of coffee in a small lounge for resident doctors. 'You're still the best theatre sister I've ever worked with.'

His compliment warmed her, but there was something in his eyes that aroused a trembling inside her which she had difficulty in controlling.

'You're the best surgeon I've ever had the honour to assist in the theatre,' she replied, and her sincerity was not feigned. 'Your technique was unfamiliar to me, but it was magnificent.'

'I had the opportunity to study various new methods in neuro-surgery while I was in Europe, and it was an experience I wouldn't have wanted to miss.'

'I know,' she murmured, looking away.

He had spoken without rancour, but tears stung her eyes even though her heart rejoiced. It was worth it! The sacrifice she had made was worth all the pain she had suffered so that he could attain perfection in his profession!

She blinked away her tears and concentrated on drinking the remainder of her coffee. Nathan was seated in an armchair with his long, powerful legs stretched out in front of him. He looked outwardly relaxed, but for some obscure reason she sensed a certain tension in him. She observed him in silence, her glance taking in his ruggedly handsome face, his sun-browned throat, the wide shoulders beneath the white, open-necked shirt, and the snake-skin belt hugging his grey glacks to his lean hips.

Nathan's physique was something she had always admired in the past, but, looking at him now, she was alarmingly aware that his physical appearance was awakening an animal attraction in her which she had never encountered before. Her mind recoiled in self-disgust, but her body had become trapped in a heated wave of desire which aroused a pleasurable, aching warmth in that part of her body which was the very essence of her womanhood.

Their eyes met unexpectedly, and shame and embarrassment sent a rush of hot blood into her cheeks when his mouth curved in a slow, sensuous smile. *He knew!* 'Don't be ridiculous!' she admonished herself, but she could not shake off that feeling that, in some uncanny way, he knew exactly what she was experiencing at that moment!

She had to get away! She got to her feet and started towards the door, knowing that she had to get away before she made an idiot of herself, but she had an awful feeling that her legs were going to cave in beneath her when she placed her mug on the table beside the stainless-steel coffee-urn.

'Are you going already?'

She could feel Nathan's eyes on her when she picked up her handbag, and her insides twitched nervously in the aftermath of what had occurred.

'It's late,' she said without turning, her jaw clenched so tightly that the words came out in a hiss between her teeth.

'So it is,' he drawled lazily. 'I'll stay a while longer to check on young Tommy before I leave.'

Julia regained a measure of her composure, and she clung to it desperately when she glanced briefly at Nathan to wish him a curt goodnight before she left.

Her heart was beating so hard and fast that she could scarcely breathe, and blind panic forced her to quicken her pace as she made her way along the well lit hospital corridors towards the reception hall. The cool night air wafted against her face when she stepped out of the building. It revived her, but she was shaking so much when she reached her car that it took several seconds to insert the key into the Toyota's ignition.

'Pull yourself together, Julia Henderson!' she reprimanded herself fiercely when nervous haste made her stall the engine, and after a second attempt she drove away without a hitch.

The familiar smell of antiseptics still hovered about her when she arrived at her cottage shortly after nine thirty that evening, and she wasted no time in stripping off her clothes and getting into a hot bath. She was tired, and the hot, scented water eased that aching tension out of her muscles, but her mind was still in a shameful turmoil.

She was not ignorant of the extent to which a woman's emotions could be aroused, but the feelings she had experienced in that small hospital lounge this evening had come close to animal lust. Her body had suddenly cried out for Nathan's with a sharp and unexpected stab of desire which she had been incapable of controlling.

Julia's cheeks flamed with remembered embarrassment, and she slid lower into the water, wishing that she could drown herself along with her shame. Did Nathan know? Had he guessed? Or had her overcharged senses heightened her imagination?

She was restless and agitated when she got out of the bath and dried herself vigorously. Oh, how she wished she could erase the memory of what had occurred with equal ease, but she couldn't, and she groaned inwardly as she slipped into her blue towelling robe and fastened the belt about her waist with a vicious tug. She took off her shower-cap, shook her hair free, and pushed her feet into soft mules before she went to the kitchen.

She was not hungry, but she had to eat something, and she boiled an egg and made herself a slice of toast and coffee. The egg and toast went down with difficulty, but she lingered at the kitchen table, enjoying her cup of coffee. She felt calmer; she was beginning to relax, but she jumped nervously minutes later when someone knocked loudly on her front door, and her glance shifted to the battery-operated clock on the kitchen dresser. *Ten thirty!*

She leapt to her feet, her nerves flaring at the sound of her chair scraping on the floor, and she walked slowly down the passage, not daring to guess at the identity of her caller, but something, a hidden instinct perhaps, was whispering one name persistently in her mind.

'Who is it?' she demanded, and she hated herself for that note of panic she heard in her voice.

'It's Nathan.'

Her pulses leapt wildly at the sound of that familiar voice, and she was breathing jerkily as she shrank away from the door. *No! She could not let him in!*

'Open the door, Julia!'

That authoritative command was sobering and, in control of herself once again, her hands reached out to lift the latch. The cool night air was heavy with the heady scent of moonflowers. It sharpened her senses, and alerted her to the alarming fact that she was naked beneath her towelling robe when Nathan stepped inside without waiting to be invited.

'What are you doing here at this hour of the night?' she demanded, her anger directed at herself rather than at Nathan.

'I wish I could say that I was passing and saw your light on, but that wouldn't be true.'

Alarm-bells rang at the back of her mind, but they grew faint when she realised that he was still wearing the same clothes he had worn at the hospital. 'Don't tell me you've been at the hospital until now?'

'I didn't want to leave until I was sure that our patient was resting comfortably.'

Julia's eyes followed the path of the hand which he raised to rub the back of his neck. He was tired and, knowing him as well as she did, she was convinced that he had been too busy going over the operation in his mind to think of having a decent meal during the day.

'Are you hungry?' she asked, the practical side of her taking charge of the situation.

'Now that you mention it, I'm starving,' he admitted, smiling guiltily, and Julia hesitated only for a fraction of a second to question the wisdom of what she was doing before she closed the door and led the way into the lounge.

'I'll make you something to eat, and then you must go home,' she said, adopting a cool, brisk manner as she walked towards the small teak cabinet in the corner of the room. 'Would you like a glass of sherry while you wait?' she asked without looking at him.

'That would be nice, thank you.'

'Sit down and relax,' she instructed, and she waited while he took off his blue blazer and lowered his tall, tired frame into a chair before she gave him the glass of sherry she had poured. 'I'll call you when the food is ready.'

Julia left him in the lounge, and she was in a feverish haste when she dashed into her bedroom to change into an old pair of lilac slacks and a faded yellow blouse. She brushed her hair into some order, and she was feeling less naked when she went into the kitchen to prepare a meal for Nathan.

She had steak grilling in the oven, and she was carrying a plate of sliced bread and cheese to the table when Nathan walked into the kitchen with his half-empty glass of sherry in his hand.

'If I stayed in the lounge much longer I might have fallen asleep,' he explained, and there was a hint of mockery in his glance when it flicked over her. 'There was no need to get dressed for me, you know.'

She flushed and turned away to concentrate on slicing a tomato into the salad she was preparing. Nathan seated himself at the table where she had laid a place for him, and she almost sliced into her finger when she felt his eyes on her. The steak was almost ready, and she broke two eggs into the pan which she had placed in readiness on the stove.

'Are you going to hire someone to take charge of the farm when you're away?' She said the first thing that came to mind in an attempt to make conversation when the silence between them started to gnaw uncomfortably at her nerves.

'I have already hired someone.'

'Honeywell was always a cattle farm.'

'I intend to keep it that way,' he replied evenly. 'What did you do about your grandmother's house in Johannesburg?'

Julia was instantly on her guard when he mentioned her grandmother, and she was wary of the questions which might follow. 'I sold the house along with most of its contents.'

'What made you decide to come to a place like Doornfield?'

'It's quiet and peaceful, and I knew that I could be happy here.'

'Are you happy, Julia?'

'Yes.' That was part truth and part lie, and she smiled derisively when she glanced at him over her shoulder. 'Did you expect me not to be?'

'I'm not sure what I expected.' Nathan's appraising glance swept critically down the length of her slender, supple body, and she could feel her skin tingle as if he had actualy touched her. 'You've lost weight, but it suits you,' he added with a sensuous smile.

She looked away quickly, incapable of sustaining his glance, but she was unnervingly aware of his eyes following every movement she made when she removed the steak from under the grill and scooped the eggs into the plate which she had warmed in the oven drawer.

'I'm afraid this is the best I can do at short notice,' she apologised at length, placing the plate of steak and eggs in front of him and casting a glance over the table to make sure that he had everything he might require.

'I appreciate the trouble you've taken, and I know this will taste good,' he smiled, buttering a slice of bread and helping himself to the tomato salad.

He ate hungrily, confirming her suspicions that he had not had a proper meal all day, and a tender, compassionate warmth stole about her heart when she turned away to switch on the electric kettle. She made coffee for both of them, and joined him at the table when he had finished eating.

'Tell me about Warren Chandler,' he steered the conversation unexpectedly in a personal direction. 'How close a friend is he?'

Julia put down her cup and her candid grey glance held his steadily. 'I've known Warren for more than two years.'

'That doesn't tell me anything,' Nathan smiled twistedly. 'Is he your lover?'

She went rigid with anger, but her glance did not waver from his. 'How can he possibly be my lover if, as you once said, I practise the art of teasing men sexually into believing that I want them only to back off before they can get me into their beds?'

Her sarcasm did not escape him, and his mouth tightened. 'That was an unforgivable statement made in anger.'

'It was,' she agreed with a forced calmness.

'Am I to understand, then, that Warren *is* your lover?'

She avoided his probing glance when she felt the tension spiral between them. 'No, Warren is *not* my lover,' she heard herself answering him truthfully.

'Is there someone else?'

'There is no one.' What was it to him anyway? He

had Marcia, what more could he want, she wondered, anger glittering in her eyes when she raised them to his. 'Why am I being subjected to all these questions, Nathan?'

'I'm merely curious.'

He smiled lazily as he leaned back in his chair, his magnetic glance holding hers, and an incredible spark of intimacy was ignited between them that made her pulses throb with a mixture of anxiety and undeniable excitement.

Damn him! Damn him for doing this to her! She had never before experienced such an emotional vulnerability, and she quivered inwardly like a hunted animal sensing danger.

'This is quite like old times, isn't it?' Nathan forced her to recall something which she had been trying desperately not to think about from the moment he had arrived. 'Do you remember how you used to make us something to eat on the evenings when we'd worked late in the theatre?'

Did she remember? Dear heaven, how could she ever forget those wonderful hours they had spent together before . . . She reined in her thoughts sharply, and wished that she could control the rapid beat of her pulses.

'I remember,' she said, her voice husky with the emotion aroused by memories best forgotten, and she lowered her lashes to veil the pain in her eyes.

'We used to close the kitchen door so as not to disturb your grandmother, and then you would concoct the most delightfully outrageous meals with whatever you could find in the refrigerator.'

There was a hint of laughter in his voice, but her

highly charged senses had picked up an undercurrent of emotion that triggered a physical response within her which she fought desperately to suppress. She did not want to reminisce about the past, but it seemed to envelop her like a heavy cloak until she felt she was being suffocated by the memory of the laughter, the dreams, and the loving they had shared. The laughter and the dreams were no longer there for her, but the love had remained against all odds. It had simmered unobtrusively in her heart all these years, and it had chosen this particular night to erupt inside her with a force which was making her body react in a way which was totally alien to her.

She risked a glance at Nathan, and wished him anywhere but there in her small kitchen. There was a strange fire smouldering in his eyes that made her catch her breath on a soft hiss, and she dragged her glance from his only to find herself staring fixedly at his unbuttoned shirt where the dark hair curled against his sun-browned chest. The desire to touch him, to feel the texture of his skin beneath her fingers, was incredibly strong, and she had to clench her hands tightly in her lap. She was in the process of being trapped by her own frenzied emotions, and she was powerless to do anything about it. The physical lure of him had been a trap of her own making. He had been aware of this, she was convinced of that, and he was playing her now on a mental leash until she would be too exhausted to deny him control.

'Drink your coffee, Nathan,' she instructed in a choked voice, rising abruptly from her chair and praying that he would leave while she was still capable of exercising some sort of control over her traunt body.

She stared down at the dishes she had piled into the sink earlier. Her hand went out to turn the tap, but Nathan seemed to materialise beside her, and his hand gripped her wrist to stay her action.

'Leave the dishes for the morning.' His free hand touched her shoulder, burning her skin through the thin cotton of her blouse when he turned her to face him. She tried to move away from him, but she was trapped against the corner cupboard. 'You're trembling and I can feel your pulse racing.'

Dear God, as if she didn't know that! His nearness and the familiar male smell of him was launching a maddening assault on her senses, and she was in deadly peril of losing that last fragile grip on her control.

He lifted the heavy strands of hair away from her flushed cheeks, and she stood petrified when his fingers stroked the sensitive skin along the column of her throat. She was almost too afraid to breathe, and her heart was hammering wildly against her ribs when he tipped her face up to his. She glimpsed her own desire mirrored in his eyes, and it robbed her of the strength to resist when he lowered his head to taste and savour her parted lips with tantalising, feather-light kisses which excited her to the point where she was aflame with a need for more. His tongue explored the soft inner flesh of her lips, and for the second time that evening a heated wave of desire engulfed her, but her mind issued a grave warning in a brief moment of sanity.

He doesn't love you! You can't want a man who is going to marry someone else! He belongs to Marcia, and don't forget it!

She leaned away from him, dragging her lips from

his and placing her hands against his broad chest to push him away, but her strength was puny, and he merely laughed at her attempt to get away from him. She was literally and figuratively cornered against the steel cupboard. There was no way of escaping unless Nathan moved aside, but something told her that he had no intention of setting her free.

'Go!' she begged frantically, her voice unrecognisably husky with emotion. 'Please go, Nathan!'

She stood powerless and rendered insensible beneath the force of her own feelings while he stroked her trembling body, and an aching warmth surged into her loins when his fingers brushed lightly against her hardened nipples.

'Why deny yourself something you know in your heart you want?' Nathan demanded thickly, a sensuous smile playing about his mouth and a slumbrous fire in his heavy-lidded eyes while he undid the buttons of her blouse with a slow deliberation. 'You want me to kiss you and touch you, and you might as well admit it.'

Her breath caught in her throat, and she gripped his wrists to stay the action of his hands. 'No!'

'No?'

His smile deepened, mocking her denial and her feeble attempt to stop him as the remaining two buttons slipped from their buttonholes beneath his fingers. She realised his wrists, blushing as she tried to cover herself, but his hands were already parting her blouse fronts to explore the smooth skin at her waist and the soft, tender swell of her breasts.

Julia's body rejoiced in the anticipated pleasure of his touch, and the voice of her conscience grew fainter.

Meeting Nathan again had been a cruel twist of fate, and she should have known that her long-suppressed emotions would be in danger of erupting at some stage. She had felt it coming all evening, like the wall of a dam bursting high up in the mountains to release a mad torrent of water, and she was trapped mercilessly at the centre of it with no control over her destination.

'Don't do this to me!' she groaned, clinging weakly to his shoulders when she realised that her treacherous body would give her no respite.

Her lashes fluttered down over eyes that had become stormy with emotion, and her head sagged back on her shoulders when Nathan's warm, exciting mouth trailed a path of fiery kisses along the curve of her exposed throat.

'Tell me the truth,' he prompted softly while his tongue explored the sensitive hollow behind her earlobe and aroused a spate of erotic sensations that made the blood leap hotly through her veins. 'That is what you want, isn't it?'

'*Yes!*' Her confession burst from her parted lips in an agonised whisper. 'Oh, God, *yes,* but it . . . it's *wrong*!'

'Look at me, Julia.' She lifted her heavy eyelids to obey him, and his fiery glance seemed to scorch hr to her soul. 'This is something we've both wanted for a long time, and it's nothing to be ashamed of.' He looked down at his hands cupping her breasts, and he drew a hissing breath. 'God knows, I've always wanted to do this to you.'

His hands shifted down to her waist, his grip firm on her flesh, and for one startled second she was airborne as he lifted her on to the cupboard so that her breasts were almost on a level with his rugged face. He lowered his head to circle one rosy nipple with his tongue before he took it into his mouth, and she gasped and trembled in the wake of that sweet, sharp stab of pleasure his touch had evoked. She slid her fingers into the short dark hair at the nape of his neck, and she was not in control of her actions when she guided his warm mouth to her other breast for a repeat of that erotic caress.

'Oh, Nathan!' she sighed jerkily, lowering her head over his, and her hair fell forward to veil her flushed, ecstatic features.

The smouldering passion in his eyes seared and excited her when he raised his head and, with an arm about her waist and the other beneath her knees, he lifted her off the cupboard and carried her from the kitchen into her bedroom.

He lowered her to her feet beside her grandmother's old double bed with the heavy mahogany headboard, and his fiery glance held hers while he lifted her blouse off her shoulders to let it slide along her arms to the carpet at their feet. 'I'm going to make love to you, Julia, and you're not going to stop me, are you?'

If there had been a tap on her emotions she might seriously have considered turning it off, but his hands were cupping her breasts, his fingers squeezing the soft mounds gently, and her clamouring body was relentless in its demand for something which only Nathan could give her.

'No,' she murmured unsteadily. 'I'm not going to stop you.'

He caught her in his arms and set his mouth on hers in a long, deep kiss that dispensed with any last fragment of doubt she might have nurtured, and her body quivered expectantly beneath his stroking hands when

he divested her of the remainder of her clothes to expose
her heated skin to the sensuous exploration of his lips
and hands. She was drowning in sensations which
aroused a throbbing, primitive need inside her, and her
surrender was total when Nathan drew away from her
unexpectedly.

'It's your turn to undress me,' he instructed throatily,
taking her hands and placing them against his chest
where she could feel the quick, heavy beat of his heart
through his shirt.

Julia felt no embarrassment as she complied with his
wishes, but she was aware of her own excitement
mounting rapidly as she undid the pearly buttons of his
shirt with trembling fingers, and slipped it off his wide,
gleaming shoulders. She would never have believed that
to undress the man she loved and wanted could be such
a sensually exciting experience. She stroked his broad
chest, loving the feel of the springy hair beneath her
palms, and the tautness of his stomach muscles.

He was lifting her hair away from her face as if to
observe every expression that flitted across her sensitive
face and, smiling faintly when she fumbled with the
buckle of his belt, he lowered his hands to help her. The
male smell of him intoxicated her, and her body was one
throbbing pulse when she exposed his lean hips and
long, muscled legs.

Her lungs felt restricted when Nathan stepped out of
his clothes and took off his shoes. His eyes were
glittering jewels of desire when he pulled her up against
his aroused body, and a choked cry escaped her as she
locked her arms about his strong neck and raised her
lips eagerly for his kiss.

'You have a body made to please a man, and I know

you're going to please me,' he murmured when he lay beside her on the bed.

Julia could not answer him while his mouth trailed fire across her sensitised skin from her breasts to her navel. Passion was a sweet madness, and a fevered moan escaped her when Nathan stroked her intimately.

Her arousal was so intense that the eventual loss of her virginity was no more than a faint discomfort swiftly forgotten in the rush of new sensations that left her mindless to everything except her mounting pleasure.

She loved him! Oh, God, how she loved this man! And *this,* it seemed, was what her body had wanted and waited for so long. Could something this beautiful be wrong? Could it?

She clung to Nathan a little wildly, her breath rasping in her throat as her excitement rose to a peak where a near-intolerable tension gripped her. Her body seemed to possess a knowledge which she had been unaware of, it moved with Nathan's in a pagan rhythm of love, and a hoarse little cry escaped her when the tension finally snapped inside her to release her from that exquisite bondage. Waves of tingling, ecstatic pleasure swept throughout her body, leaving her sated and contented—for the moment—to the very depths of her soul as she welcomed the shuddering weight of Nathan's body on hers. She held him tightly, reluctant to end this moment of closeness, and they lay with their bodies entwined until the heavy beat of their hearts subsided.

Nathan moved his face against her throat, she could feel the roughness of his beard against her skin, and she was overawed at the thought of what they had shared. A warm feeling erupted inside her, it burst from her heart in a rush until the words, *I love you,* hovered perilously on her lips, but she bit them back hastily when Nathan stirred and eased himself away from her.

His face was in shadow when he raised himself on to his elbow to look at her, but the dim bedside light behind him was sufficient for her to see that he was smiling at her for the first time without that familiar glint of mockery in her eyes, and her eyes filled with tears.

'I'm glad I was the first after all,' he murmured, his hand stroking her thighs and trailing across her flat stomach to fondle her breasts with gentle fingers.

Julia was too happy at that moment to take exception to his remark, and her hand went up to touch his cheek when he leaned forward to brush the tip of her small, straight nose with his lips before his mouth found hers in a lingering kiss. She was also too busy trying to analyse her own thoughts and feelings, but Nathan's warm mouth was moving against hers with an urgent sensuality that made it difficult for her to think coherently, and she finally relinquished the effort to surrender herself to the pleasure of his touch. Nothing else seemed to matter now except this closeness she was sharing with the man she loved, and the voice of her conscience had diminished to an inaudible whisper.

CHAPTER SEVEN

THE shrill, persistent ringing of the alarm clock was an unwelcome intrusion on Julia's dreams, and she groaned protestingly as she flung out an arm to silence it. She stifled a yawn behind her fingers and stretched lazily, wishing that she could stay in bed a while longr, but then, suddenly, she remembered. Her breath locked in her throat, and she sat up in bed with a jolt, jerking the sheet up against her naked body, but she need not have bothered. Nathan's clothes were gone, and the silence in the cottage indicated that she was alone.

Julia sat staring straight ahead of her, almost too afraid to think, and then she saw the note which had been propped up against the jar of night cream on her dressing-table. She leapt out of bed and, dragging the sheet with her across the room, she snatched up the note and read it.

My apologies for leaving so early. I took the liberty of using your telephone to call the hospital. I was told that Tommy Durandt had a reasonably peaceful night, but I'm driving out to the farm for a shower and a change of clothing before going to the hospital to check on him personally. I'll see you this evening, if not before. Nathan.

Julia sat down heavily on the dressing-table stool, and she went cold and hot in rapid succession as she recalled every intimate detail of what had occurred between Nathan and her during the night. They had made love

119

fiercely and passionately, and then they had made love again, but that second journey towards fulfilment had been a long and leisurely experience which had left them both sated. The last thing she could remember was lying in his arms with her head on his shoulder and her legs still entwined with his.

It had all seemed so perfect last night. Her love for him had been the overriding factor, it had justified her actions, but in the cold light of day the memory of what had occurred filled her with shame and a deep sense of guilt. She took refuge in anger, but her fury was directed at herself for having had so little control over her emotions. What, for God's sake, must Nathan think of her? She had lost all sense of decency in order to assuage the desire of her flesh and, for someone who ought to know better, she had also been extraordinarily careless. She had not paused once to consider the possibility that she might become pregnant! And what about Marcia? Julia was merciless on herself as she drove the sword of condemnation into her soul by changing places mentally with Marcia, and she felt sick and disgusted with herself as she flung Nathan's note to the floor to bury her quivering face in her hands.

She had spent the night with a man who she had known was going to marry another woman, and she could not blame Nathan for her indiscretion. She had wanted him, and he had sensed it. Her love for him had made her an easy prey, but loving him was not a sufficient excuse for what she had done, and it did not erase that terrible feeling of guilt. Oh, if only she had had the strength last night to put a stop to something which she should have known she would regret deeply in the morning! If only . . .!

Julia had difficulty in concentrating on her work that day, and on two occasions Roland had cause to reprimand her severely for not carrying out a simple instruction.

'What's the matter with you, Julia?' he questioned her when he entered the deserted waiting-room late that afternoon and seated himself on the corner of her desk. 'You're not your usual self today.'

'I'm sorry, Roland,' she sighed ruefully, clearing away the remaining files on her desk and lowering herself tiredly into her chair. 'It must be the after-effects of a rather disturbing night.'

Roland lifted his heavy eyebrows anxiously behind his gold-rimmed spectacles. 'I was given to understand that the operation on Tommy Durandt went off very well.'

'Oh, it did!' she assured him hastily.

'What is it, then?'

A shadow flitted across her face and she looked away. 'It's a personal matter.'

'I see.' There was an awkward little silence before Roland changed the subject. 'What did it feel like to be working in the theatre again?'

Julia surfaced from those painful and embarrassing memories which had plagued her all day. 'It was marvellous experience!'

A smile plucked at Roland's mouth, but his eyes were grave. 'Are you thinking of leaving me for a job at the hospital?'

'No!' She shrank inwardly at the mere thought of it as her candid glance met his. 'You've been good to me, Roland, You *and* Elizabeth, and I'm very happy working for you. Oh, I admit it was exciting to be able to work in a theatre again, but I like it here with you, and I mean that sincerely.'

'I'm relieved to hear that.' A speculative look entered his eyes. 'I saw Nathan on my early-morning rounds at the hospital, and we discussed Tommy Durandt's post-operative treatment among other things.'

'What other things?' she demanded nervously, her body tensing and her hands tightening their grip on the arms of her chair.

'*You*, mainly.'

'You discussed *me*?' she echoed faintly.

'Don't look so anxious, my dear,' he smiled down into her wide grey eyes. 'Nathan asked questions about you, but I told him nothing which he could not have heard from any number of people in the village.' He gazed at her intently for a moment, then he sighed exasperatedly. 'Don't you think it's time you told him the truth, Julia?'

'I *can*'t!' There was an ache in the back of her throat and her voice was husky with the effort to speak. 'The reason why I ended our engagement five years ago is no longer of importance.'

'Why not?'

She lowered her gaze and swallowed hard. 'He's going to marry Marcia Grant.'

'Did Nathan tell you this?'

She shook her head tiredly. 'Marcia told me.'

Roland was silent for a moment, then he rose to his feet and sighed once again. 'Well, it's time to go home, and I hope I'm going to have an undisturbed night.'

Julia echoed that wish for herself as she picked up her bag and followed him out of the building, but she somehow doubted that her mind would allow her a moment's peace.

She drove home with mixed feelings that afternoon. She craved the solitude of her small cottage, but she also dreaded it, and she knew the reason for her contradictory feelings when she finally unlocked her door and walked down the short passage to her bedroom. The memory of what had occurred there the previous evening was still too fresh in her mind, and Nathan's presence seemed to linger there like a phantom, haunting and tormenting.

She deposited her handbag on the dressing-table and kicked off her shoes to walk in stockinged feet to the kitchen to make herself a cup of coffee. She tried to fill her mind with mundane things, such as what she would have for dinner that evening, but the thought of food made her insides curdle in rejection, and her thoughts returned promptly to Nathan. He had said in his note that he would see her this evening, if not before, and she had lived with the dread that he might walk into the waiting-room at any time during the day. How was she going to avoid seeing him that evening? She could switch off her lights and pretend to be out, but sitting there in the dark while Nathan hammered on her door was not something that appealed to her.

The coffee did not steady her, it simply stimulated her mind into a state of panic, and she kept herself occupied preparing a meal which she knew she would be incapable of eating. She had to do *something* if she did not want her thoughts to drive her crazy.

She prepared something light, something which she hoped would slip down without too much effort, but in the end she merely rearranged the order of the food on her plate. She was tense and nervous while she waited for that dreaded knock on her door. She prayed it would not come, and she almost leapt out of her skin when the telephone started ringing.

That would be Warren, she thought, succeeding in calming herself. He had promised to give her a call from Durban. But she almost dropped the receiver when she heard Nathan's deep, well modulated voice saying, 'I thought I'd let you know that I have a few things to look into here at the farm before I see you this evening.'

Julia was not sure afterwards whether it had taken seconds or several minutes for her to control herself sufficiently to speak, but she was grateful that Nathan was not there to witness the way she was shaking.

'I would prefer it if you didn't come here this evening.'

There was a brief but ominous silence at the other end before Nathan said, 'May I know why?'

'I'm really very tired, Nathan, and I—I'd like to have an early night,' she replied, closing her eyes in silent prayer as she leaned back against the wall for support.

'I promise not to stay long.'

'No!' Her voice sounded sharp, almost panicky, and she lowered it hastily to inject a note of calmness into it. 'Some other time, perhaps, but not this evening. I'm tired, I want to be alone, and I have a lot of thinking to do.'

'I have to leave for Johannesburg in the morning, and I don't expect to return to Doornfield before the weekend,' he informed her brusquely. 'I was hoping we could have a talk before I left.'

'We'll talk when you're back.'

'Very well, but . . . about last night, Julia. I don't want you to get the idea that I——'

'*Please,* Nathan!' she interrupted him hastily, her heart beating painfully in her chest. he did not have to underline the fact that last night had meant infinitely more to her than it had to him. He had wanted her, but his love belonged to someone else, and she had no illusions about that. 'I said we would talk when you get back,' she added coldly.

There was a stony silence on the line before Nathan ended the conversation with an abrupt, 'Right! I'll see you at the weekend.'

The dialling-tone purred in her ear, and she drew a

jerky breath as she lowered the receiver on to its cradle. She blinked away the tears that pricked her eyelids, but she could not rid herself of that ache in the back of her throat, and she was still hovering beside the telephone, swallowing convulsively, when it rang again.

Julia flinched away from the instrument on the table beside her, and she stared at it as if it were a viper about to strike her. It rang for several seconds before she scraped together sufficient courage to answer it, and her relief was so intense when she discovered it was Warren at the other end of the line that she almost burst into tears.

If Warren had heard the thickness of unshed tears in her voice he made no mention of it, but she wasted no time in controlling herself.

'I miss you,' he said at length, and she was uncomfortably aware that there was more to that statement than she could cope with at the moment. 'Is there any hope for me, Julia?'

She should have said, 'No, there isn't, but she recalled Roland de Necker's warning that she could not go through life shutting her heart to other men. She had to face the fact that there was no hope for her with Nathan and, if she was honest with herself, she would have to admit that she liked Warren very much. He loved her, and he would be a wonderful husband, but she was still having difficulty reconciling herself to the knowledge that she would be marrying a man she did not love.

'I wish I could say "yes", Warren, but I can't. Not yet, anyway,' she added quickly when she realised that her reply might be interpreted as a rejection.

'I guess I shall have to be patient a while longer, won't I,' he sighed disappointedly, but there was a smile in his voice that warmed her cold heart.

'I'm afraid so, Warren,' she replied dismally, hating herself for what she was doing to him. 'How are you progressing with the preparations for your sister's wedding?' she asked, steering their conversation on to safer ground.

'Everything's going smoothly.'

Their conversation ended some minutes later on a light and impersonal note, but Julia lapsed into a sombre, depressed mood when she returned to the kitchen. She scraped her untouched meal into the bin, and piled the dishes into the sink to wash them, but her mind was not on what she was doing. She was thinking about Nathan, and she was recalling his remark on the telephone which she had interrupted for fear of hearing his rejection, but she could not rid her mind of those words.

'I don't want you to get the idea that I . . .' *Love you?* What else could he have intended to say? He was going to marry Marcia, and last night had meant nothing to him. Julia cringed inwardly at the memory of what had occurred. She had made it obvious that she was available and willing, and Nathan had not allowed this opportunity to slip through his fingers. He had made love to the woman who had jilted him five years ago, and what sweet justice it must have been from him to avenge himself in that way.

I'm glad I was the first after all. Nathan's remark slipped unbidden into her mind, and it strengthened that painful conviction that his actions had been prompted by the desire for revenge.

Julia pulled out the plug and clutched the side of the sink with her soapy hands. That ache was still there in the back of her throat, and this time she could not prevent the tears that spilled on to her cheeks. *Dammit,* she was not going to cry! She dried her hands and

snatched up a paper towel to dab furiously at her eyes
and her cheeks. She had Warren who loved her and
wanted to marry her, and she owed it to him to give his
proposal of marriage a great deal more serious thought.
It was senseless to deprive herself of a home and a
family of her own simply because she could not have the
man she wanted!

Julia enjoyed working in her garden. It was also a form
of therapy to her that Saturday afternoon, and it helped
her to relax after a particularly trying and soul-
destroying week. She was thinking about Warren while
she kneeled on the grass to loosen the soil between the
seedlings she had planted along the fence, and she was
hoping that she would see him on his return to
Doornfield the following day, but her thoughts were
interrupted when a car stopped outside her gate.

She looked up, and she could almost swear that her
heart turned over in her breast at the sight of Nathan
getting out of his Ferrari. The gate swung open beneath
his hands on well oiled hinges, and he smiled faintly
when he saw her.

'Hello, Julia.'

Her heart was thudding against her ribs when she sat
back on her heels and looked a long way up into those
incredibly blue eyes which she knew would haunt her
until the end of her days. He was dressed casually in a
cotton short-sleeved shirt, and his brown slacks were
styled to perfection to draw attention to his lean hips
and long, muscular legs. The rich, creamy colour of his
shirt accentuated his tanned complexion and heightened
his masculine appeal, but she cursed herself silently
when she felt that familiar stirring of her senses.

'You're frowning,' Nathan observed with a gleam of
amusement in his eyes. 'Am I to believe that I'm not

welcome?'

She thrust her small garden fork into the loose soil and stood up, aware suddenly of her appearance when she saw his glance taking in her bare feet, faded T-shirt and denims, and the dilapidated, wide-brimmed straw hat which she had planted firmly on her head to protect her face and neck from the blistering rays of the sun.

'I had planned to spend the afternoon gardening, and I wasn't expecting visitors,' she explained, her cheeks flushed with annoyance. 'Would you care for a glass of fruit juice?'

Nathan nodded, a quizzical look in his eyes, and she gestured towards the garden table and chairs beneath the trees. Common sense had warned that there was danger in being alone with him in the cottage, and she waited for him to be seated before she pulled off her garden gloves and went inside.

She was shaking inwardly, and her heart was beating much too fast when she took the jug of fruit juice out of the refrigerator and placed it on a tray with two tall glasses. The ice tinkled in the glass jug when she carried the tray out into the garden where Nathan sat stretched out in one of her garden chairs, and he looked up with a lazy smile that made her pulses leap wildly in response. Stay calm! Julia warned herself as she placed the tray on the table. For God's sake, control yourself!

She poured their drinks with an admirably steady hand, and passed him a glass with a casual, 'I hope you like it.'

Nathan sipped at his drink and raised his eyebrows. 'It has a refreshing taste. What is it?'

'Fresh orange juice with a dash of lemon and soda.' She flung her straw hat on to the empty chair beside her and observed him unobtrusively while she drank thirstily from her glass. 'I always find it refreshing when I'm working in the garden on a hot day such as this.'

His glance rested briefly on her hair which she had tied back with a scarf in the nape of her neck, and she glimpsed that hateful gleam of amusement in his eyes once again before he turned his head to look about him appreciatively.

It was a scorching day with hardly a breeze stirring the air, and the atmosphere was strained and tense between them, despite the peace and tranquillity which Julia's garden had to offer. What was he thinking about? she wondered cynically, stealing a glance at Nathan's stern, handsome profile while they drank their cold drink, and her insides coiled into an agonising knot. She knew the reason for this visit. He wanted to be sure that she had not misconstrued his reasons for making love to her.

'About the other night,' she began stiffly when she could no longer tolerate the tension in the air between them. 'I want you to know that I blame myself entirely. It was something which should not have happened, and it must *never* happen again.'

He turned his head to look at her, his eyes narrowed and faintly mocking in the dappled sunlight. 'Do you expect me to believe that?'

'Yes, I do.'

'Why, Julia?'

For some obscure reason he was being deliberately obtuse, and she flashed him an angry glance when she leaned forward to place her empty glass on the tray, but she had to look away the next instant when she felt the unexpected sting of tears behind her eyelids.

'You should know the answer to that better than I do,' she rebuked him in a voice that was not as steady as she would have wished.

'Should I?' The wooden chair creaked beneath his weight and she heard the faint thud of his glass joining hers on the tray. 'Does this have any connection with the reason why you broke off our engagement five years ago?'

Anger came to her rescue, and she blinked away her tears to glance at him sharply. 'You know it doesn't!'

'No, I *don't* know.' He spoke calmly, but there was something ominous in the set of his strong jaw. 'What was your reason for not wanting to marry me?'

'I believe you have asked me that question before, and my answer is still the same.' She avoided his penetrating glance to stare down at her bare feet, and anxiety made her curl her toes into the soft grass. 'I didn't love you enough to marry you.'

'You didn't love enough to marry me, but you still want me, and you proved that when you allowed me to make love to you.'

That was a sobering statement. Her head shot up as if she had been jerked by the hair, and her cheeks flamed at the memory of how eager and willing she had been in his arms. His glance trailed down her body with a slow deliberation, and a sensuous smile curved his mouth to make her suspect that he was mentally stripping her of her clothes and enjoying the experience. She wished that she could run and hide, but it was too late now for a display of modesty when there was not an inch of her body which Nathan had not explored with his lips and hands during those hours of passion they had shared.

She pulled herself together with an effort and shrugged with an affected casualness. 'You don't have to love a man to want him.'

'That doesn't apply to you, Julia,' he contradicted her with a mocking laugh. 'You're a woman who could never entrust your body to a man if you didn't love him.'

'Don't be ridiculous!' she exclaimed, a suffocating sensation settling in her chest at the fear of Nathan's discovering the extent of her feelings and holding them up for ridicule.

'If I'm judging you incorrectly, then I'd like you to explain why you were still a virgin.'

'I—it was——' She halted her stammering reply and resorted to anger as her only defence. 'Nathan, I don't have to explain anything to you, and I wish you would go away and leave me alone!'

'I'm not leaving until I've received satisfactory answers to a few pertinent questions I intend to put to you,' he responded, the set of his jaw relentless.

'Oh, really?'

'What was the cause of your grandmother's death?' he demanded, ignoring her sarcasm.

'She had cancer,' she answered abruptly, knowing the futility of lying to him when a simple investigation would have revealed the information he was seeking.

'Was that why you decided not to marry me? Because you felt you were under an obligation to stay and nurse her through to the end?'

Julia stared at him, mentally winded by the accuracy of his assumption, and the deep timbre of his voice had an ominous ring to it that sent a shiver of fear racing through her. This was not the moment for confessions, she was not emotionally prepared for it, and she rose to her feet with a jerky movement.

'I'm not in the mood for this inquisition,' she flung at him coldly, picking up the tray and carrying it into the cottage to escape him, but he followed her inside.

'What's the matter, Julia?' he demanded with a derisive smile when they stood facing each other with the width of the small kitchen table between them. 'Am

I getting too close to the truth for comfort?'

The kitchen walls seemed to be closing in on her, suffocating her, and her lips parted to draw a gulping breath. Oh, how easy it would be to tell him everything he wanted to know, but she was no longer sure how he would react. The years between had changed him as much as it had changed her, and raking up the past was not going to solve anything. A few nights ago she had conveniently ignored the fact that he was going to marry Marcia Grant, but she was not going to forget it again to add to that burden of guilt which she knew she would carry with her for the rest of her life. No, she was never going to forget it again! *Never!*

'Go away, Nathan!' She turned her back on him to stare blindly out of the window with her hands clenching the edge of the cupboard. 'Go away and leave me in peace!'

'I'm tired of these evasions, and I'm fast approaching the limit of my patience!'

His soft-soled suede shoes had made no sound on the tiled floor to warn her of his approach, and she was caught totally unprepared when she was spun round by the shoulders to face him. He glimpsed the sheen of helpless tears in her eyes, and he muttered something unintelligible as he caught her in his arms and crushed her against the hard length of his body. Wide-eyed and startled, her lips parted in protest, but the words were smothered beneath that hard mouth which had descended on hers.

A wave of dizziness engulfed her, and she clutched at his shoulders to steady herself, but her instinctive action was taken as encouragement. Nathan's mouth softened and moved against hers with a sensuality that assulted her senses, and she could feel her control slipping precariously when his hands shifted up beneath her

T-shirt to trail a path of destruction along the sensitive hollow of her back. Her resistance was crumbling swiftly when his mouth left hers to seek out the pulsating hollow of her throat, and she wanted him so badly at that moment that she trembled with the force of her emotions, but she came to her senses when she felt the catch of her bra give way beneath his fingers.

She struggled desperately to free herself. Her hands were flat against his broad chest in an attempt to push him away, and her breath was beginning to rasp in her throat when his hands cupped her breasts.

'No!' she gasped, and fear was her motivation as she thrust him from her with a burst of strength she had not known she possessed. 'Don't do this to me!'

'I want you, Julia,' he murmured throatily, his desire to learn the truth temporarily set aside. 'I want you, and I know you want me.'

'No! I don't want you!'

His smouldering eyes flashed in anger. 'You're lying, and I'll prove it to you!'

She knew she would be lost if he touched her again, and she darted away from him, placing the kitchen table between them before he could reach for her.

'Aren't you forgetting something?' she said coldly. 'Aren't you forgetting about Marcia?'

'Marcia?' he demanded with a harshness that made her wince inwardly. 'What has Marcia got to do with this?'

His callous disregard of the woman he was going to marry left Julia momentarily shaken. Was it possible that someone could change so much in five years? Did he feel nothing at the thought of betraying Marcia's trust?

'She has *everything* to do with this! Julia exclaimed, her anger rising to a peak where she felt like striking him.

Nathan stared at her as if he thought she had taken leave of her senses, then he gestured dismissively with his hands. 'Marcia and I are——'

'I don't want to know about your past, present, or future relationship with Marcia Grant,' she interrupted him, furious and also curiously disappointed. 'All I want at this moment is for you to get out of here, and I don't want you ever to come back. I want to be free of you, Nathan, as free as I was before you barged back into my life a few weeks ago, and I hope you will have the decency to respect my wishes.'

She was turning that savage knife in her own heart with every word she uttered, but she had no choice, and the ensuing silence was so intense that her raw nerves jarred at the sound of a dove cooing in the tree outside the kitchen window. Nathan had gone strangely white about the mouth, and his eyes blazed into hers with an anger that frightened her, but her glance did not waver from his. She dared not look away now if she wanted to lend credibility to her statement.

An agonising eternity seemed to pass before Nathan spun round and walked away from her with long, angry strides. Julia stood as if she had become rooted to the tiled floor beneath her bare feet, and it was only when she heard his car drive away that the terrible tension snapped inside her. She collapsed into a chair, and buried her face in her arms with a convulsive sob.

CHAPTER EIGHT

THERE had been clear indications since the beginning of the week that the weather was building up towards a storm. The bushveld heat was oppressive, and the Thursday morning had scarcely begun when Julia could feel the perspiration breaking out all over her body beneath her cool white uniform. It was going to be another of those long, hot summer days, and she sighed resignedly as she got up to adjust the position of the fan on the filing-cabinet to give Roland's wilting patients the maximum benefit of the breeze produced by those madly whirling blades.

Julia thumbed through the files on her desk, but she did so automatically. She was thinking about Nathan. Almost a week had passed since the Saturday afternoon when she had had the temerity to order him out of her cottage, and out of her life. She doubted that she would ever forget the icy anger that had replaced that look of incredulity of his face, and her heart still mourned her actions, but it had been the only thing to do if she wanted to maintain what was left of her tattered self-respect.

She reined in her painful thoughts when the consulting-room door opened and an elderly farmer emerged, leaning heavily on a sturdy cane for support. He raised his hat and they exchanged smiles when he passed her deak and, glancing at the appointment book, Julia selected the appropriate file and rose behind her desk to usher the next patient into the consulting-room.

Roland's manner was calm and pleasant, but Julia could see the lines of weariness and growing irritation etched about his mouth when he called her into the consulting-room to assist with the ante-natal examination of a young woman. The unbearable heat was robbing him of his usual stamina, and Julia could sympathise with him while she was locked in a desperate battle with herself to ward off that lethargic feeling which had been threatening to engulf her since early that morning. She was looking forward to her lunch-break when she would join Warren at his restaurant for a quiet, relaxing meal, but the hours seemed to drag tediously that morning.

'God knows I feel my age today,' Roland laughed wearily when the waiting-room had cleared, and he lowered himself into the chair behind her desk, stretching his legs out in front of him. 'I have never before longed with such intensity for a morning to end.'

Julia turned from the filing cabinet to smile at him, and her grey glance softened with compassion. 'This heat is enough to sap anyone's strength.'

'Is it time to close up shop?' he asked as if he was simply too tired to lift his arm to look at his wristwatch, and she glanced beyond him at the electric clock against the wall.

'Do you think anyone will complain if we leave the surgery five minutes early?'

'*I* certainly shan't complain,' he grunted, gripping the arms of the chair to lever himself up on to his feet. 'Get your things and let's go.'

Julia opened her handbag to make a few hasty repairs to her appearance while Roland disappeared into the consulting-room to take off his white jacket and collect his bag. She was taking a critical look at herself in her powder-compact's small, circular mirror and brushing a stray strand of hair behind her left ear when Roland returned, and he eyed her speculatively when she closed the compact and dropped it into her handbag.

'Are you going home for lunch?' he asked her when she preceded him out of the room and out of the building into the blazing heat of the sun.

'I'm meeting Warren.'

'You've been seeing quite a lot of Warren Chandler lately.' Roland pocketed his keys, and his eyebrows were raised in a quizzical arch when he glanced at her. 'Is there something on the go that I don't know about?'

'I've always liked Warren, and I enjoy his company,' she answered him evasively. 'I'm afraid that's all there is to know about our relationship at the moment.

Roland muttered something unintelligible as they walked round the whitewashed building to where they had garaged their cars, and they parted company in silence.

The interior of Julia's car was like an oven despite the fact that it had been parked in the shade, and she wound down the window in the hope of catching a breeze while she drove down the main street of the village towards the Mopani restaurant. A thick layer of clouds had gathered over the mountains in the distance, but this had been a regular occurrence for the past five days without bringing Doornfield the relief its inhabitants sought.

The Mopani restaurant stood shimmering in the heat like an oasis in the desert when Julia drove up to it and parked her car beneath a shady tree. The sun was merciless, it stung her face and arms as she weaved her way among the outdoor tables towards the entrance, but the air-conditioned interior of the building had the effect of a cool cloth against a fevered brow, and she breathed a sigh of relief, pausing for a moment simply to enjoy the cool air wafting about her before she made her way towards the table at the rear of the restaurant where she knew she would find Warren.

'I'm glad you could come, Julia,' he smiled at her when she was seated facing him across the circular table. 'Shall we order immediately?'

She smiled and nodded. 'I think that would be advisable. I don't want to be late for work.'

Julia hastily scanned the menu he had give her. Warren ordered a grilled sole, but she prefered a salad dish, and they sat for some time without speaking after Joseph had left with their order. The silence between them did not trouble Julia; she was finding pleasure in simply taking the weight off her feet, and relaxing to the soft strains of the music which was relayed into the restaurant.

'You look exhausted,' Warren remarked at length with concern, and his dark glance lingered on the shadows beneath her eyes which her make-up had failed to conceal.

'It's this heat,' she explained away the evidence of her sleepless nights. 'I wish it would rain.'

Warren grimaced playfully. 'When it rains the restaurant business unfortunately suffers.'

'I never thought of the rain in those terms,' she laughed softly, spreading her hands in a helpless gesture. 'It's impossible, of course, to please everyone all the time.'

'You're beautiful when you laugh.' His expression was grave when he reached across the table to capture her hand in his. 'You don't laugh often enough, my dear.'

She wished that she could think of something witty to say, but her mind remained uncomfortably blank, and her expression sobered as she stared down at his fingers curling about hers on the table. Oh, if only his touch did not leave her so absolutely cold.

'Nathan Corbett's lady-friend is back in town.' Warren's unexpected announcement made her body stiffen in a painful spasm as if her nerves had made contact with a high-voltage wire. 'He called about an hour ago to book a table for two this evening.'

Julia eased her hand out of Warren's clasp, and she schooled her features into a blank mask before she raised her face to meet his dark glance across the table. 'I have no interest whatsoever in the activities of Nathan Corbett and his lady-friend.'

'That sounds promising!'

There was something in Warren's smile that made her feel uneasy, and he leaned towards her as if he wished to pursue that topic of conversation, but Joseph chose that moment to arrive at their table with their lunch.

Julia sighed inwardly with relief, and stared down at the salad dish she had ordered. It had been tastefully prepared, but her appetite had dwindled into oblivion at the knowledge that Marcia Grant was staying out at Honeywell with Nathan. Would this agony never end?

'I received a letter from my mother and she says she's looking forward to meeting you,' Warren interrupted her thoughts, and she raised startled eyes to his.

'You told her about me?'

'You were seldom out of my thoughts, and I had to explain the reason for my preoccupation,' he smiled self-consciously, putting down his knife and fork and leaning towards her earnestly. 'What about spending a few days in Durban with me some time next month?'

Julia shied away from the thought of meeting his family. It might suggest that there was something in their relationship which she was not sure she would ever be ready for, and it would simply make things awkward if his family jumped to the wrong conclusion.

'I'm not due for leave until November,' she prevaricated.

'I'm sure that Dr de Necker wouldn't object to giving you a few days' leave if you asked him.'

She felt as if she was being driven into a corner, and she imagined that it showed on her face. 'I don't suppose he would object, but . . .'

'Hey, Julia!' he interrupted her cautious reply when he sensed the reason for her hesitancy. 'Meeting my family doesn't mean you're under an obligation to marry me!'

She coloured slightly and lowered her gaze to her plate. 'What did you tell your mother about me?'

'I told her everything except the fact that I'm in love with you and want to marry you.'

'It wouldn't surprise me if she worked that out for herself,' she remarked drily, risking a glance at him, and encountering a gleam of mischief in his eyes.

'I've raved about other women in the past, but I never married any of them.'

'Oh, Warren!' she sighed helplessly, a smile plucking at the corners of her soft mouth.

'Eat your salad before it goes limp on your plate,' he advised with mock severity, and Julia was forced to make a pretence of eating.

She was not looking forward to leaving the cool interior of the Mopani restaurant, and it appeared as if most of the diners shared her reluctance. She had watched them linger over one cup of coffee after the other, and she wished that she could do the same, but the minute hand of her wrist watch was moving relentlessly towards two o'clock.

'I have to go,' she said at length, dabbing at her lips with her table napkin and picking up her handbag.

'I was serious about taking you down to Durban with me for a few days, and I hope you'll give it some thought,' Warren said when he accompanied her out of the restaurant.

'I'll consider it,' she promised when they stepped out of the building, and she grimaced when the heat washed up against her as if she had stepped too close to a veld fire.

'Will you let me know? Soon?'

'Soon,' she nodded, but she knew in her heart what her answer would be.

She could not accompany him on a visit to his family. She also had clarity about something else. She could never marry Warren. She was fond of him, and she appreciated his friendship, but that was all it would ever be.

Julia was in a saddened and disturbed state of mind when she drove away from the restaurant. Her future lay before her like a barren wasteland, but she could not marry Warren while her heart belonged to Nathan. She could not be so cruel to someone as nice as Warren, and she could not live with him as his wife knowing that the shadow of her love for Nathan would always be there between them. It would drive her insane, and it would destroy Warren.

The heat had reached its peak the Sunday of that same week, but there was still no sign of rain. Julia felt as if she was wilting like the flowers in her garden, and she had barely had sufficient energy that afternoon to wash her luncheon dishes and stash them away. She had toyed with the desire to take a nap, but she had known that she would not sleep, and to lie down would merely aggravate that lethargic feeling in her limbs. She was wondering how she was going to pass the time when the ringing of the telephone pierced the stifling silence in the cottage, and it seemed to take a considerable effort to get up and answer it.

'Come over for tea,' Elizabeth de Necker invited. 'Roland has gone off to the hospital, and I am in desperate need of company.'

Julia heaved an inward sigh of relief. Here, at last, was something to do, and she accepted Elizabeth's invitation without delay. 'Give me half an hour to change into something decent.'

She sponged her face in cold water, and changed into a cool, lemon-coloured frock which left her shoulders bare except for the narrow straps holding up the bodice. She applied a light touch of make-up, and left her shoulder-length hair free of the confining combs. Nathan had always liked it that way. But she did not *want* to think about Nathan!'

It had taken her half an hour, almost to the second, to reach Elizabeth and Roland de Necker's home. She parked her car beneath a shady jacaranda tree in the street, and she was walking up the curved path towards the entrance of the house when Elizabeth stepped out on to the porch with its attractive assortment of potted plants.

'I'm so glad you could come,' she smiled, linking her arm through Julia's, and drawing her into the air-conditioned interior of the house. 'It's miserable sitting here all alone on a Sunday afternoon, and I wondered if you might not also be in need of company.'

'I had planned to spend the day with Warren, but something cropped up at the last minute and he had to cancel,' Julia explained as they entered the spacious, restfully furnished living-room where a tray of tea and scones had been laid out on the low, square table which stood between two comfortably padded chairs.

Elizabeth poured their tea into those delicately flowered china cups she loved, and she tempted Julia with a plate of freshly baked scones. They relaxed in their chairs while they drank their tea and talked. Elizabeth was not a taxing person to be with. Her conversation was intelligent but never demanding. She was, however, quick to assess a situation, and her shrewd brown eyes seldom missed anything.

'You're not looking well, Julia,' she observed gravely when the teapot was empty and the scones on the plate had dwindled to a few. 'The last time I saw you looking like this was three years ago when you arrived in Doornfield.'

Julia could not speak. It felt as if someone had seized her by the throat, and she hid the torment in her eyes by fixing her gaze on her tightly clasped hands.

'You're still in love with Nathan Corbett.' Elizabeth's astuteness drew a strangled gasp from Julia, and she could not suppress the tears in her eyes when she met the older woman's glance. 'Oh, you poor, dear girl!' Elizabeth murmured, shaking her head. 'And it must be absolute *hell* knowing that he is going to marry someone else.'

Her compassion and understanding intensified that aching lump in Julia's throat, and she swallowed convulsively as she brushed the tears from her eyes with the tips of her fingers. 'I'll survive,' she said, looking away.

I'll survive! Those two words were beginning to sound like a perfect epitaph to Julia. Five years ago she had said *I'll survive*. She was saying it again now, but this time it was not going to be so easy. Self-pity? No, she dared not pity herself! If she was going to survive, then she dared not start by pitying herself! She succeeded in regaining her composure to some extent, but she could not rid herself of that lead weight which had settled in her chest.

'Are we going to lose you?' Elizabeth queried at length, her troubled glance drawing Julia's.

'I don't think I could stay on here in Doornfield knowing that I might periodically bump into Nathan and his . . . wife.' Her voice broke, but she controlled herself and smiled twistedly. 'That's a little too much to expect of me, don't you think?'

'Don't do anything hasty, my dear,' Elizabeth warned gently. 'Nathan hasn't married that woman yet.'

Julia remained silent. Elizabeth was offering her hope where there was none. Nathan was going to marry Marcia, Marcia had made no secret of that, and Julia was determined not to stand in his way. What, after all, did she have to offer a man like Nathan in comparison with what Marcia and her father could offer him?

The sound of a car coming up the driveway interrupted her anguished thoughts, and seconds later she was alerted to the fact that a second car was entering the driveway.

'That must be Roland,' Elizabeth smiled, rising and walking across to the window which looked out on the driveway. 'I must say he had returned home earlier than I expected, and—oh, dear!' She dropped the lace curtain into position as if it had stung her, and her expression was clouded with concern when she glanced at Julia. 'He has Nathan and that woman with him.'

Julia paled visibly, and she rose jerkily from her chair with a panicky desire to run. She could slip out of the side door before they entered the house, but then she remembered that her car was parked at the front gate. It could not have escaped their notice, and she would only succeed in making herself look foolish by running like a scared rabbit.

'Elizabeth!'

Roland's voice was raised as if he was attempting to warn them of something which they had discovered for themselves. Julia's pulse-rate accelerated to a suffocating pace, and her fingers curled spasmodically into her damp palms, her nails digging painfully into the soft flesh.

'In here, dear!' Elizabeth answered him, exchanging a quick, reassuring glance with Julia before Roland entered the living-room with Nathan and Marcia following close behind him.

'I bumped into Nathan and Marcia at the hospital and invited them home for a cup of tea,' Roland explained, casting a brief but apologetic glance in Julia's direction before he made the necessary introductions. 'Marcia, I would like you to meet my wife. Elizabeth, Marcia Grant.'

'I'm so pleased to meet you, Mrs de Necker.'

Marcia's husky voice was honeyed, but Julia was not aware of Elizabeth's response when, for one electrifying second, she found herself staring into Nathan's angry blue eyes.

'You know Julia Henderson, don't you, Marcia?' Roland was saying, and Julia's back felt rigid when she wrenched her eyes from Nathan's to meet Marcia's dark, speculative glance.

'Yes, we've met before,' Marcia smiled sweetly, but there was a calculating coldness in the look she gave Julia.

'Make yourselves comfortable while I switch on the kettle and make a fresh pot of tea,' Elizabeth said, breaking the strained and tense silence which seemed to hover like an ominous cloud in the living-room.

'I'll help you, Elizabeth,' Julia offered hastily,

seizing this opportunity to escape for a few minutes to regain her composure and, picking up the tea-tray, she followed the older woman out of the living-room with the feeling that two pairs of eyes, in particular, were setting fire to her back.

'I'm so sorry, my dear,' Elizabeth apologised in a hushed voice when they were alone in the kitchen. 'I know how awkward and unpleasant this must be for you, and I wish Roland had telephoned home before arriving here so unexpectedly with that woman in tow.'

'Please don't concern youself,' Julia reassured her with a shaky smile. 'It would look odd if I left now, so I'll stay long enough to have a quick cup of tea.'

'Oh, dear! The afternoon has somehow been ruined for me!'

'Nonsense!' Julia rebuked the older woman gently, stepping forward to offer her assistance. 'Here, let me rinse out the cups for you, and I'll prepare the tray if you'll tell me where you keep the rest of these cups.'

'You'll find the matching cups in that cupboard behind you,' Elizabeth told her, filling the kettle before plugging it into the wall socket and switching it on.

Helping Elizabeth in the kitchen had a claming effect on Julia, but she was disturbingly aware of the murmur of voices in the living-room. Marcia's tinkling laughter seemed to punctuate their conversation, and it grated across Julia's raw nerves. She did not want to think; she did not want to feel, but her mind persisted in conjuring up a vision of Marcia's seductive body in white slacks and lime-green top, and she could not help recalling how Marci had slipped a possessive arm through Nathan's as if to stress the fact that he was her exclusive property.

Please, God, she prayed silently. Why do I have to spend the rest of my life wanting a man who no longer loves me? And why do I find it so difficult to believe that Marcia can make him happy?

'Are you ready?' Elizabeth intruded on her agonising thoughts some minutes later, and Julia forced her stiff lips into a smile.

'I'm as ready as I'll ever be.'

'Good girl!'

Elizabeth picked up th tray of tea and scones, and Julia braced herself mentally when she followed the older woman from the kitchen.

'May I take that for you?' Nathan offered politely, rising when they entered the living-room, and Julia's heart seemed to take a painful leap into her throat at the height and breadth of him in his immaculate grey slacks and the blue, short-sleeved shirt which seemed to span too tightly across his powerful chest.

'I can manage, thank you, Nathan,' Elizabeth smiled up at him pleasantly as she brushed aside his offer of assistance. 'I'll deposit the tray here on the low table, and you may all help yourselves when I have poured.'

Nathan resumed his seat on the padded sofa beside Marcia, and Elizabeth seated herself behind the marble-topped table where she could pour their tea in comfort. Julia lowered herself into a chair beside Roland, and the smile he bestowed on her was warm and somehow comforting.

'You have a delightful home, Mrs de Necker.' Marcia broke the awkward silence while they helped themselves to a cup of tea and a scone. 'I especially admire the way you have succeeded in blending the old with the new. This is the type of décor which is the most fashionable at the moment in Johannesburg.'

'The choice of décor has come about by accident rather than design,' Elizabeth explained with a coolness in her voice which Marcia might have been unaware of, but it did not escape Julia. 'My aim has always been to create a comfortable, lived-in home in which my husband could relax when his patients allowed him a little time to himself.'

'People in the medical profession have to work such unholy hours at times, but that, thank goodness, shan't apply to you, darling.' Marcia smiled at Nathan and placed a carefully manicured, possessive hand on his thigh before she explained her statement to Roland and Elizabeth. 'My father wants Nathan to take charge of the surgical section of the new clinic which is being erected in Johannesburg, and I'm happy to say that it will require a regular eight-to-five day which will leave Nathan free in the evenings as well as weekends.'

Roland raised his eyebrows behind his gold-rimmed spectacles, and there was a hint of disapproval in his eyes which did not match the smile that curved his mouth. 'It sounds like a posh job, Nathan.'

'It's going to be a posh clinic when it's completed,' Nathan responded in a clipped voice, and Julia could not be sure, but she sensed a lack of enthusiasm which might suggest that his values had not changed as much as she had imagined.

'Is this post at the clinic a certainty?' Elizabeth asked Nathan in a display of polite interest, breaking the ensuing silence which threatened to become awkward.

'I've received a legitimate offer, but I still have plenty of time to inform them of my decision.'

Nathan's glance met Julia's briefly while he spoke, and she was shaken by that flash of blazing fury she had glimpsed in his eyes before he looked away. Why was he still so angry with her? Surely he had enough sense of decency left to know that what they had done was wrong, and that she had acted in their best interests when she had ordered him out of her cottage?

'My father says that Nathan would be a fool not to accept this post, and Nathan is very much aware of that,' Marcia's honeyed voice interrupted Julia's disturbing thoughts. 'This new clinic will be equipped and staffed to make it the best in the country.'

And the most expensive, Julia could not help thinking with a measure of distaste as she recalled her conversation with Damian Squires, and she felt sick inside when she sensed Roland and Elizabeth's disapproval.

'Thank you for a lovely afternoon, Elizabeth, but it's time I went home,' Julia announced with a desperate need to get away, and she placed her cup in the tray as she rose to her feet.

'I'll walk with you to your car, my dear,' Elizabeth smiled at her, and there was something in her eyes that made Julia suspect that Elizabeth was equally anxious to escape for a moment.

Julia received a curt nod from Nathan and a cold stare from Marcia, but Roland surprised her by drawing her towards him and kissing her on the cheek in much the same way a father might greet a daughter. A warmth filtered into her cold heart, and her step was lighter when she walked out of the house with Elizabeth. The late afternoon sun lengthened the shadows of the trees across the well kept lawn, and Julia drew the clean, fresh air deep into her lungs in an attempt to ease that feeling of suffocation which she had encountered from the moment Nathan and Marcia had entered the house with Roland.

'It seemed as though Marcia and her father have Nathan's future mapped out very nicely for him, and Nathan doesn't appear to object too much to the idea of being manipulated, but I imagine that it's one way of making a name for oneself,' Elizabeth remarked with a wry smile when they walked down the curved path towards the gate where Julia had parked her car.

'I don't think the situation is quite what Marcia Grant would want us to believe.' Julia leapt to Nathan's defence before she could prevent herself. 'I knew Nathan as a man who was interested solely in the improvement of his skills as a neuro-surgeon in order to heal those who came to him for help. Making a name for himself was never one of his ambitions.'

Elizabeth's attractive features wore a dubious expression, and there was a hint of pity in her eyes when she glanced at Julia. 'People change, my dear.'

'I know,' Julia agreed as she paused at the gate to face Elizabeth. 'People change, but I find it difficult to believe that one's sense of values could alter to such a drastic extent.'

'I hope you are right about Nathan,' Elizabeth responded gravely. 'It would be a relief to know that my first assessment of his character was still intact.'

Julia drove home in a sombre, pain-filled mood. She had stood aside five years ago because she had wanted Nathan to achieve the heights in his profession, and she was doing the same now. He was going to marry Marcia Grant, and Marcia, with the assistance of her father, could help him achieve notoriety. Was that what Nathan wanted? Was it possible that making a name for himself had become more important to him than the desire to heal with the skilful wielding of his scalpel?

CHAPTER NINE

IT was almost two weeks since that Sunday afternoon when Roland had arrived at his home accompanied by the two people whom Julia had wished to avoid at all costs. It had rained for several days, making the gravel roads in and around Doornfield almost impassable, but it was not the weather which had aroused this strange uneasiness in Julia as the days flowed one into the other. She had an odd feeling that she was sitting on the edge of a volcano which was threatening to erupt, and she was unsettled by the knowledge that there was nothing she could do to stop it.

Roland de Necker appeared to mirror her wariness and intense irritation when she walked into his consulting-room after lunch the Wednesday afternoon to find him seated behind his desk, drumming his fingers impatiently on his desk blotter.

'Is something the matter?' she asked him cautiously.

'It's nothing that can't wait,' he said abruptly, leaning back in his chair and making a visible attempt to relax. 'I needed to discuss Tommy Durandt's progress with Nathan, but when I telephoned Honeywell I was told that Nathan has been in Johannesburg for the past two days,' he explained when Julia continued to stare at him curiously.

'Is Tommy Durandt not responding to treatment as well as you had expected?' she asked with a calmness that belied the nervous and bitter turmoil inside her at the mention of Nathan's name.

151

'My concern is not for the patient,' Roland announced, taking off his spectacles and cleaning them with unnecessary vigour before he put them on again and pocketed his handkerchief. 'It's just that I'm baffled that Nathan should go off like that when he had stated quite emphatically that he would be available for consultation any day of this week.'

'He must have been called away to something important.' Julia heard herself proffering an excuse for Nathan's absence, but she had to admit to herself that his contradictory behaviour was odd.

'Perhaps you're right,' Roland agreed, dismissing the subject with a characteristic wave of the hand. 'You may send in the first patient.'

She did as she was told, but that brief conversation with Roland had left her in a disturbed state of mind beneath her outwardly calm and smiling exterior. Why had Nathan gone to Johannesburg when he had told Roland that he would be available for consultation any day during this week? Was Marcia Grant perhaps the cause of this unexpected trip to the city?

Julia needed to relax, and she had settled herself comfortably in her lounge that evening with a book she had been wanting to read for some time, but her mind wandered repeatedly. Why had fate been so unkind as to bring Nathan back into her life to disrupt the peaceful existence she had created for herself? During the past two weeks she had suffered the agony of thinking that she might be pregnant, and then there had been the relief of discovering that she had been mistaken. Relief had, however, given way to regret, and an acute and inexplicable bout of depression had followed which she was still having difficulty in shaking off. It was ridiculous to have felt so deprived, she rebuked herself sensibly, and she was attempting once again to concentrate on her book when she heard a car driving up the lane and stopping at her gate.

It was Nathan! She had recognised the sound of the Ferrari's engine, and her body tensed when she heard Nathan's heavy footsteps approaching the cottage. His knock on the door jarred her nerves, and her legs were shaking beneath her when she rose to her feet.

Her heart was thudding nervously against her ribs when she opened the door, but her breath locked in her throat when she confronted Nathan's tall frame on her doorstep. His face looked grim, and the grooves stretching from his nose to his strongly chiselled mouth had deepened with obvious exhaustion. The jacket of his grey suit was draped carelessly over his arm, the sleeves of his white shirt were rolled up to above his elbows, and he had loosened his collar and tie. Tenderness and compassion rose like a tidal wave inside her, but she suppressed it hastily. She dared not soften now!

'May I come in?' he asked, his deep, well modulated voice intruding on her distracted thoughts, and his sensuous mouth quirking in a suggestion of a smile which was not mirrored in his heavy-lidded eyes.

'I'd prefer it if you didn't,' she responded with a rudeness which was alien to her nature, and there was a stabbing flash of anger in his blue glance.

'Dammit, Julia, I've spent two aggravating and exhausting days in Johannesburg, I haven't been to the farm yet for a much-needed shower and a change of clothing, and I'm not in the mood to tolerate this kind of treatment from you!'

She backed away hastily when he stepped inside, but fingers of steel bit into the soft flesh above her elbow as he closed the door and propelled her into the lounge where he flung his jacket on to the nearest chair.

'Let go of me!' she gasped.

Nathan was hurting her, but it was nothing compared to the pain he inflicted when he took her shoulders in a merciless grip and jerked her round to face him. His eyes blazed down into hers with a frightening anger, and she swallowed convulsively, stilling beneath his punishing hands.

'I don't know what game you think you're playing, Julia, but it has got to stop!' he warned savagely.

Game? If anyone was playing a game, then it was Nathan! A numb pain shot down into her arms, and she winced inwardly, but her glance did not waver from his.

'I'm not in the habit of playing games.'

'Aren't you?' he demanded with a grating harshness, and she was released with an unexpectedness that made her stagger and clutch at the back of a chair for support. 'You allow me to make love to you; you *welcomed* it, in fact, but when we meet again I'm given the cold shoulder. *Why,* Julia?'

'It was the sensible thing to do, for your sake as well as my own.'

Nathan's eyes narrowed perceptibly. 'Could you be more explicit?'

Dear God! How could she explain the guilt and the mental torment she had suffered without making him realise that she still loved him? No, she dared not even attempt an explanation, she decided as she snatched at the first reasonable explanation that came to mind.

'Warren has asked me to marry him, and I——'

'You can't marry Warren Chandler!' Nathan interrupted her with a savagery which she had never encountered in him before, and she paled visibly as she backed a pace away from him, but her eyes sparked with a defensive anger when she met his glance.

'I'm free to marry whomever I please, and you have

no right to tell me that I——'

'You don't love him!'

Her heart lurched violently in her breast, but her angry glance did not waver from his for an instant. 'Since when have you become an authority on my feelings?'

'You love *me,* Julia!' he answered her with that unfamiliar savagery, and it felt as if her heart and lungs had come to a grinding halt inside her.

She could feel the last vestige of blood drain away from her face to leave it cold and clammy, and she fought desperately against that perilous darkness which threatened to engulf her. The last thing she wanted at that moment was to collapse in a heap at Nathan's feet.

'You're *crazy!*' she cried hoarsely, shuddering inwardly as her vitals resumed their normal function.

'Am I crazy, Julia?' he smiled twistedly, his eyes glittering with a hateful mockery as he jerked off his tie and undid a few extra buttons down the front of his shirt to expose his powerful chest with the matting of dark hair against his tanned skin. 'Would you rather have me believe that when we made love it was a purely physical act for you, and nothing more?'

'It *was* just a physical thing!' she lied frantically.

'You're a bad liar, my dear Julia.' His smile deepened with derision. 'You always were, and you always will be.'

She cast caution aside in her desperate attempt to conceal her true feelings. 'You're planning to marry Marcia, so why can't you leave me alone!'

A muscle leapt in his jaw and a terrifying look entered his eyes. 'Who told you that I was going to marry Marcia?'

Julia cursed herself silently for not keeping her mouth shut about what she knew, but it was too late now to retract her statement, and she swallowed nervously, knowing that only the truth would suffice under these distressing circumstances.

'Marcia implied as much during our conversation that night when Damian took me out to your farm, and she didn't deny it when I questioned her for clarification,' Julia explained, her voice husky with the effort to force the words past the tightness in her throat.

'And you were more than ready to assume that I was planning to marry her,' Nathan accused harshly, flinging her mind into complete confusion.

'Aren't you?' she asked, deliberately quelling that flame of hope which had been ignited inside her. 'Aren't you planning to marry Marcia?'

'My God!' Nathan exploded savagely, and fear clutched at her chest and stilled the breath in her throat when he raised his hands as if he intended to choke her, but he controlled himself and let them drop to his sides again. 'You haven't credited me with the slightest sense of decency, have you! You simply took it for granted that I was capable of making love to one woman while at the same time I was contemplating marriage to another!'

'I had no reason to believe that she was lying to me, so why shouldn't I have assumed that you were going to marry her?' she parried his accusation with an indignant anger which helped to deaden the pain inside her. 'You have been seeing Marcia for the past year, and everyone knows that she has spent a considerable amount of time with you at Honeywell since you bought the farm.'

Nathan's glance sharpened, and the probing intensity of his gaze heightened her wariness and placed her on her guard. 'Have you been jealous?'

'Don't be ridiculous!' she snapped, turning from him in a fury which was directed mainly at herself when she felt that tell-tale warmth sliding into her cheek.

It was true . . . *dammit*! Jealousy had been gnawing away at her like a cancer these past weeks, but she was not yet ready to admit it to him while she was still in the vice-like grip of a rampaging uncertainty.

'You're the only woman I have ever proposed marriage to. What made you opt out at the last minute, Julia?'

She should have known that this verbal altercation would lead to an interrogation, but she had been too busy attempting to cope with the bewildering discovery that Nathan was not planning to marry Marcia, and his probing query had been delivered with the unexpectedness of an electric shock. It jolted her nerves violently, and it left her momentarily numb.

'I'm almost convinced that it wasn't because you stopped loving me, so I've concluded that there had to be another reason,' he persisted when she remained silent, and his voice had an ominous ring to it that made the blood chill in her veins.

'Go away, Nathan!' she said through her teeth, shaking in every limb and close to breaking-point as she gripped the back of a chair once again to steady herself. 'For God's sake, go away and leave me in peace!'

She had that terrible feeling again that she was sitting on the edge of a volcano, but this time she knew it was going to erupt, and she was panic-stricken at the knowledge that she could do nothing to stop it.

'Julia . . .'

'*No!*' She brushed off his hand when he touched her shoulder, and her face was white and pinched when she spun round to face him. '*Leave me alone!*'

The atmosphere between them was heavily charged as they stood facing each other like opponents locked in a deadly battle of wits, and the unrelenting set of

Nathan's jaw filled Julia with the awesome suspicion that she was going to be the loser.

'I deserve to know the truth, Julia. I'm entitled to it, and I demand an explanation *now!*'

Nathan's command made her shrink inwardly, but she was forced to recall something which Damian Squires had said. 'You've got to tell Nathan the truth. It might make him human again instead of the insufferable, unreasonable man he has become.'

An intense weariness seeped into her body, and she could feel her rigid resolve crumbling. It was as if she had walked a long, exhausting distance which had robbed her of the stamina to contemplate taking another step. If Nathan wanted the truth, then she no longer had the strength to withhold it from him, and she was simply too tired to care about the consequences.

Her shoulders sagged wearily, and she walked away from his glaring appraisal to stare blindly out of the window with eyes that were dark with the pain of remembering.

'Julia?'

'Yes, yes, I'll tell you what you want to know. It doesn't matter any more, and I——' She halted abruptly to rid herself of that aching restriction in her throat, and it took a few moments for her to control herself sufficiently before she could continue speaking. 'A few weeks before our wedding I—I was told that my grandmother had cancer and, when I considered all the sacrifices she had made for me, I felt I owed it to her to—to stay and nurse her through those last two years of her life.'

The ensuing silence was so intense that Julia was convinced Nathan could hear the painful pounding of her heart, and her mouth was suddenly so dry that her tongue was threatening to cling to her palate.

'Why didn't you tell me this five years ago?'

The hint of incredulity in his voice made her turn, but his features were etched in a black fury that quickened the pace of her heart with fear, and she leaned back against the window-sill to support her body on trembling legs.

'What would you have done if I had confided in you, Nathan?' she counter-questioned.

'I most certainly wouldn't have allowed you to bear that terrible burden on your own.' His tight-lipped reply did not come as a surprise to her; it was what she had always known he would say, but the confirmation of her suspicions was of little comfort to her. 'We could have been married,' he added, 'and I would have postponed my study-trip to Europe.'

'Opportunities like that don't come along every day, Nathan. We both know it,' she smiled mirthlessly, 'and I didn't want to stand in your way.'

'My God!' He crossed the room in a few long strides, and she shrank back against the window at the menace in his stance when he towered over her. 'So you broke off our engagement almost on the eve of our wedding, and left me to believe the worst of you!'

'I had no choice.'

'The choice to stay or go should have been *mine,* not *yours*! For God's sake, Julia!' His hands shot out, and she cried out in fear when he took her by the shoulders and shook her until it felt as if her neck was in danger of snapping. 'You had no right—no right whatsoever—to make a decision like that on *my* behalf!'

'I did what I thought was best for you!' She choked out the words, and he thrust her aside with a force that made her stagger back against the polished window-sill.

'Best for *me*? *Dammit!*' His harsh voice grated along raw nerves, and she raised her wary glance to see him run his fingers through his hair in a furious gesture before he pinned her down with a blazing glance that made her quake inwardly. 'Do you have any idea what I went through when I received that polite and uninformative note of yours telling me that the wedding was off? Does it matter to you that when I couldn't contact you I nearly went out of my mind trying to find a reasonable explanation for your actions, or don't you care at all?'

Dear God, how could he ask her that? She cared more than he could ever know, and her actions in the past had been motivated solely by her love and concern for him! The pain of it all washed over her, tearing cruelly at her soul as she recalled the hours and the days of agonising torment which had finally led to her decision to sever their relationship. She had always been convinced that she had made the right decision; it was that thought which had sustained her during the past five years, but now she was begining to think that she might have been wrong, and that Nathan had every reason to be furious with her.

'I'm sorry,' she apologised lamely, her voice a husky whisper with the effort to force the words past that aching tightness in her throat.

'Is that all you can say?' he demanded harshly.

She looked up to encounter the fiery anger in his probing eyes, but a numbness was taking hold of her, and it robbed her of the ability to feel and think coherently.

'What else is there to say?' she croaked.

Nathan's lips drew back in a snarling fury, and a stab of icy terror succeeded in penetrating that blanket of numbness which surrounded her.

'My God, I could——'

He broke off abruptly, and Julia had a blurred vision of his menacing features when he pulled her roughly and unexpectedly into his arms to set his mouth on hers in a brutal kiss that crushed her soft lips against her teeth. The agony of it made her want to cry out, but the sound was stifled in her aching throat, and hot tears welled up behind her closed eyelids.

This was a punishment which Julia knew she would not forget in a hurry. Her arms were pinned helplessly at her sides, and her breasts were hurting against his hard chest. Any attempt to escape this ruthless embrace would merely have intensified the pain, and it was the numb acceptance of the punishment he was dishing out that made her body yield against his. Her soul was beginning to feel as bruised as her body, but the most painful of all was the dawning suspicion that she deserved it.

Nathan's furious assault could not have lasted for more than a few seconds, but it felt as if an eternity had elapsed before she was released to stand swaying dazedly on her feet with the distinct taste of blood in her mouth. She could not see his features clearly through her tears, but she heard him curse throatily before he stalked out of the cottage and slammed the door behind him with a force that made the windows rattle.

Julia could not sleep that night. She tossed for hours while her mind worked its way repeatedly through everything that had occurred that evening. How could something which had once seemed so right suddenly appear to be so wrong? She was too confused and bewildered to find the answer to that question, but most of all she was labouring under a feeling of guilt which was making her squirm inwardly.

During that storm of soul-searching and self-reproach there was one vital and tantalising piece of information which she had overlooked, and it was not until the early hours of the following morning that she found herself recalling Nathan's accusation that she had not credited him with a sense of decency. 'You simply took it for granted that I was capable of making love to one woman while at the same time I was contemplating marriage to another,' he had said. What, exactly, had he meant by that? And what about Marcia? Had there been no truth at all in Marcia's statement that she and Nathan were going to be married?

Julia's mind was too exhausted to reason, and she finally drifted into a troubled sleep from which she awoke three hours later with the feeling that she had a head which was twice its normal size. She groaned and had to drag herself out of bed to get herself ready for work. Her temples were pounding, and the day loomed ahead of her like an unassailable mountain. Her headache abated after she had swallowed down a couple of tablets with a cup of coffee, but there was nothing she could do about her tender, bruised lips, and she winced several times when she applied her lipstick.

If Roland noticed during his busy daily schedule that something was amiss, then he made no mention of it, but Julia was relieved when he left the consulting-rooms that afternoon to keep an appointment with Nathan at the hospital, and the door had barely closed behind his tall frame before she took advantage of the fact that she was alone to lean back in the chair behind her desk with a tired sigh. She felt drained, and the cool, pleasant mask which she had been forced to wear all day was slipping to reveal her hollow-eyed exhaustion. She wanted to go home. She needed to catch up on the hours of lost sleep, but, more than that, she needed time alone to think.

Julia's hopes for a quiet evening alone at home were dashed when Warren arrived at her cottage shortly after seven thirty. She was not in the mood for company, but she resigned herself to it when she recalled that there was an important matter which had to be settled between them, and the sooner she settled it, the better for both of them.

She made coffee and took it through to the lounge where Warren coaxed her on to the cane bench beside him. They talked quietly while they drank their coffee, and Julia somehow succeeded in keeping their conversation on an impersonal level while she waited for the right moment to broach the subject she had to discuss with him, but she knew that she could not delay the inevitable when Warren made an attempt to take her into his arms.

'There is something I have to tell you, Warren,' she began, her voice husky with regret and self-reproach as she gently warded off his embrace, and the pained expression on his face made her look away guiltily. 'I want you to know that I'm deeply honoured by your proposal of marriage, and I've considered it most seriously these past weeks, but I—I know now that I can't marry you. It was wrong of me to allow you to hope for something which I've known all along would never work. I'm fond of you, I really am, but I couldn't marry you without loving you.'

'I've been expecting this,' Warren announced without rancour, but there was a hint of bitterness in the smile that curved his mouth. 'It's Nathan Corbett, isn't it? You're still in love with him.'

He was not asking a question, he was making a statement which did not require an answer, and her gaze fell before his. It was true; she *was* still in love with Nathan, and she had always known that no other man could ever measure up sufficiently to take his place in her life.

'I'm sorry, Warren,' she murmured ruefully, hating herself for allowing their relationship to progress as far as it had, and she wished there was some way she could ease the pain for him. 'You've been a good friend, and I thank you for that.'

An awkward silence followed, and she sat staring miserably at the carpet beneath her feet when she sensed his disappointment and anger. He had every right to be annoyed with her, and she would not blame him if he chose to berate her for leading him on along a path which she had known from the start could lead nowhere, but he surprised her by taking her hand in his and raising it to his lips.

'I would like always to be there for you as a friend, and if you need me you only have to call.' He was smiling when he released her hand and rose to his feet, but the smile did not quite reach his dark eyes when he stood looking down at her. 'Remember that, Julia.'

He was gone before she could say anything, and she was still sitting there in the lounge long after she heard him drive away. She was weeping silent tears, but she could not decide whether her tears were for Warren, or for herself. She had sent him out of her life because of her feelings for Nathan, but Nathan had not come, and now she had no one.

Julia arrived home shortly after one on the Saturday afternoon, and she was garaging her car when she heard her telephone ringing. Nathan? She rushed inside to answer it, but it stopped ringing a fraction of a second before she lifted the receiver, and she bit her lip nervously as she frowned down at the instrument. It rang again a few seconds later, and she snatched up the receiver, but that flicker of hope in her heart was doused when she recognised Damian Squires's gravelly voice.

'I have news for you,' he said without preamble, and an odd tremor raced through her. 'I've heard from a reliable source that Nathan has declined the position Basil Grant offered him at that fancy new clinic.'

'I doubt if that will please Marcia. I wonder how it will affect their relationship.'

She wished she hadn't said that, but it was too late now, and she held her breath mentally as she waited for Damian to speak.

'I think their relationship ended a long time ago for Nathan, but Marcia's very good at hanging on to what she's got and, knowing Nathan, he simply didn't bother to do anything about it until now.'

'Why now?' she asked, her heart beating in her throat and making it difficult for her to speak. 'If you suspect that he has ended their relationship, then what would have made him end it now?'

'I was hoping you could tell me.'

Julia was not quite sure how she ought to respond to that remark. Her thoughts and her feelings had been flung into a chaotic state, and she was too wary to grasp at something which she feared might disintegrate the moment she touched it. Her future had suddenly taken on the appearance of a fragile soap-bubble which was floating and hovering rather precariously over a thorn tree, and she could not decide what to do about it.

'Have you told Nathan the truth?' Damian intruded on her thoughts, and it took a few frantic seconds to gather her scattered wits about her to realise what he was referring to.

'Yes, I've told him.'

'And?' Damian prompted after a significant pause.

It was not difficult to call to mind Nathan's reaction when she had confronted him with the truth. Every word, every inflection in his voice, and every expression which had flitted across his ruggedly handsome face had been branded as if with fire into her memory. It haunted her day and night, and she doubted if it would ever cease to make her cringe inwardly.

'Nathan was furious with me,' she confessed, her grey eyes shadowed, and her throat aching. She swallowed convulsively, and fingered her lips as if she still expected to find them bruised and tender after Nathan's savage punishment. 'He said that I had had no right to make a decision like that on his behalf, and . . . do you know something, Damian? . . . it makes terrifying sense.'

'You did what you considered was best for him at the time.'

Damian's prompt and confident reply to her statement was endearing, but it did little to comfort her while she laboured under that dense shadow of self-reproach.

'I'm relieved to know that you're still of that opinion.' The words had passed her lips on a shaky laugh, but she controlled herself hastily when she felt her eyes stinging with those tears which seemed to come so easily since her last confrontation with Nathan, and her face was set in a rigid mask of determination not to weep when she continued speaking. 'I feel as if I've made such a mess of everything, and I doubt if Nathan will ever forgive me. He stormed out of here in a filthy mood the other night, and I haven't seen him or heard from him since. What am I going to do, Damian?'

'I'm not sure I can advise you on that, but whatever you do, Julia, you'll have to do it quickly,' Damian warned her gravely. 'Nathan is due back in Johannesburg within a couple of days to take up the reins of his practice and, knowing his busy schedule, it might be some time before you see him again.'

'Thank you, Damian.'

She wondered what she had thanked him for when she eventually replaced the receiver. The next move was hers; that was something which she had begun to realise during those long, sleepless nights of self-recrimination and, as Damian had said, she had better move quickly.

Nathan deserved to be told the complete truth— she owed it to him as well as herself—but she dreaded the thought of having to confront him. Circumstances had forced her to hurt him badly five years ago, and the explanation he had wrung from her had merely set fire to his anger and that understandable bitterness which had obviously been simmering inside him all these years. She had no guarantee that Nathan still cared for her, and she feared the humiliation she would be subjected to if his interest in her had been motivated solely by the desire for revenge, but it was up to her to discover where she stood with him, or she might regret it for the rest of her life.

Julia's telephone rang again later that afternoon, and she was startled into silence when Marcia Grant's voice exploded into her ear with an icy fury.

'I don't know if you're aware of it, but Nathan has decided against taking the position my father offered him at the clinic, and you're to blame for that!'

Marcia's accusation caught Julia unawares, but she regained her composure swiftly. 'I fail to see how I could have influenced Nathan's decision when the subject has never been discussed between us on the few occasions we have met.'

'He has made a grave mistake in rejecting my father's offer. He's throwing away a chance in a lifetime, and I know he'll regret it,' Marcia continued in those icy tones. 'If you don't want to have this on your conscience for the rest of your life, then you'll sacrifice your selfish desires and see to it that he is made aware of his error.'

Sacrifice? Julia fought down that fierce wave of hysteria which rose sharply inside her. 'I've spent the best part of my life sacrificing my own happiness for Nathan's career,' Julia informed Marcia coldly, 'but everything has its limits, and this time I refuse to step aside if there's a chance that happiness should come my way.'

'If you're hoping that Nathan will ask you to marry him, then you're making the same mistake I made,' Marcia laughed mockingly. 'His interest in women no longer includes a trip to the altar, and I don't somehow think you're the type who would agree to live with a man without a wedding band on your finger. I don't want to prevent you from trying, but don't say that I didn't warn you of the outcome.'

Marcia's mocking laughter was still ringing in Julia's ears long after she had replaced the receiver, and she was more determined than ever now to take that contemplated drive out to Honeywell to settle matters one way or the other between Nathan and herself.

CHAPTER TEN

THE wind was blowing the dust into a swirling red mist which was trapped in the beams of the Toyota's headlights, and the first heavy drops of rain splattered on to the windscreen as Julia turned her car off the gravel road to drive through the arched gateway which led to Honeywell. There was a twist of anxiety in her stomach, but she ignored it stoically. She had left her cottage that Saturday evening with a purpose in mind, and she was not going to turn back now. She didn't know whether there was anything left to salvage between Nathan and herself, but she would never forgive herself if she did not make the effort.

There were grazing camps on either side of the farm track. In the darkness she caught a glimpse of the new wire fencing which Nathan had had erected since her previous visit, but she was too busy concentrating on her driving to see much else. The rain had changed the dust to mud on the windscreen, and the wipers were swishing back and forth in a frantic attempt to allow Julia sufficient visibility. She could see lights up ahead through the trees, and her hands were clenched so tightly around the steering-wheel that her fingers were aching when she finally drove up towards the stone building with its pillared veranda.

'This is it!' she muttered to herself when she pulled up behind Nathan's red Ferrari which was parked beside the shallow steps leading up to the entrance of the house.

Julia dropped her keys into her handbag and, getting out of her car, she dashed quickly through the rain, but her beige slacks and blue silk blouse felt uncomfortably damp against her skin when she reached the cover of the darkened veranda. The light was on in the hall, she could see it through the stained-glass windows on either side of the ornately carved door, and she felt again that twist of anxiety in her stomach when she smoothed her hair into place and rang the doorbell.

The door was flung open several seconds later, and Julia's heart lurched uncomfortably when she came face to face with Nathan. His dark hair lay damply across his broad forehead as if he had just stepped out of the shower, his white shirt was unbuttoned almost to his waist, and his brown slacks seemed to be moulded to his lean hips and long, muscular legs. He stared at her without speaking, and her courage almost deserted her when she noticed that there was no sign of welcome on his granite-hard face.

'This is unexpected,' he said at length, his cold glance raking down the length of her slender body and up again to where the agitated rise and fall of her breasts was clearly visible beneath the silk of her blouse.

There was nothing complimentary in his lingering appraisal, and she prayed nervously that he would not see that frightened little pulse throbbing at the base of her throat, but there was a mixture of desperation and defiance in the tilt of her head while she stood regarding him steadily with her clear grey eyes.

'I didn't think to make an appointment. Do you mind?' she asked as a flash of lightning illuminated his face, and her glance registered the fact that his features looked grim and haggard. 'We have to talk, Nathan.'

For one frantic second she thought that she was going to have the door slammed in her face, and she sighed inwardly with relief when he stood aside for her to enter, but she sensed a controlled anger in him when he gestured her into the living-room with an autocratic wave of his hand.

'May I pour you a sherry?' he offered to the accompaniment of the thundering elements outside, and Julia felt oddly as if she had stepped into the den of a ferocious lion, but she had not come this far only to give way to cowardly feelings.

Stay calm, she warned herself sternly. For God's sake, stay calm and don't let him guess how nervous you are!

'A sherry would be nice, thank you,' she replied, her voice admirably steady, but her insides were shaking when he walked away from her towards the drinks cabinet.

Julia strolled around the spacious living-room, listening to the rain dripping down the gutters and attempting to ease the tension inside her by admiring the paintings on the walls, but the beauty of the landscapes on canvas escaped her when she failed to quell her rising panic. It had been a mistake to arrive at Honeywell uninvited, and she was recalling only too vividly the unpleasantness of her previous visit when she heard a step behind her. She pulled herself together, turning slowly, and her facial muscles were rigid with the control she exercised when she accepted the small glass of sherry from Nathan.

'Cheers!' he said, lowering his tall frame into a chair and saluting her with his glass of whisky when he had stretched his long legs out in front of him.

'Cheers,' she echoed dully, perching nervously on the edge of an armchair some distance from his, and swallowing down a mouthful of her sherry to steady herself while she watched Nathan down more than half the contents of his glass in one gulp.

The ensuing silence was strained and incredibly tense, and it was disconcerting to discover that her glance was straying repeatedly to where his unbuttoned shirt exposed his powerful chest with that dark matting of hair tapering seductively down towards his navel.

Despite Nathan's chilly aloofness he was exuding an aura of raw masculinity which was attacking her senses and, unnerved and disorientated, she said the first thing that came to mind. 'I believe you're returning to Johannesburg within a couple of days.'

She could have bitten off her tongue the next instant when she realised what she had said. Nathan must know that only one person could have given her that information, and she might just as well have mentioned Damian by name.

'I have a job to get back to,' he reminded her, his eyes mocking her, and she looked away hastily to cast a nervous glance about the room.

'I like the alterations you've made to this old house.'

'Do you, Julia?'

Dammit! She didn't drive all the way out to Honeywell to indulge in this meaningless conversation with Nathan. She was wasting precious time, but he was not giving her the encouragement she had hoped for, and the words she wanted to say remained locked away inside her. She pressed on despite that twisting ache in her stomach. 'I suppose you see Honeywell as a retreat you can escape to on the occasional weekend when you can get away from the city.'

'That was what I had in mind when I decided to buy the place.' He swallowed down the remainder of his whisky, and there was a hint of derision in his narrowed, mocking eyes when he placed his empty glass on the low, glass-topped table beside his chair. 'Shall we cut the preliminaries and get down to the reason for this unexpected visit?'

When do you leave?'

'First thing Monday morning.'

His departure was suddenly so imminent tht she felt choked with anxiety. He was right, it was time to cut the preliminaries, and she dared not waste another second.

'I received a telephone call from Marcia late this afternoon.' If she had hoped for some sort of reaction from Nathan, then she was disappointed. His features remained inscrutable, and she was forced to continue. 'She told me that you had decided against accepting her father's offer of a senior post at the clinic.'

'That's correct.'

Julia sipped at her sherry to steady her nerves while she tried to decide how much she ought to tell him, but something warned her that it would be safer not to hide anything from him.

'For some obscure reason Marcia accused me of influencing your decision, and she insisted that it was up to me to make you change your mind since she was convinced that you would regret passing up this opportunity.' She glanced at him warily. 'I know this is none of my business, but I thought you ought to know.'

'You're right, it's none of your business,' he said harshly, getting up to pour himself another drink, 'but since Marcia has seen fit to involve you I might as well set the record straight. I declined Basil Grant's magnanimous offer for the simple reason that I have no desire to become a celebrated puppet, and this is not a decision I shall have cause to regret. As for Marcia saying that you influenced my decision, well . . .' he shrugged and smiled cynically as he returned to his chair '. . . it's a typical reaction from a woman who is having difficulty coping with not getting what she wants.'

That made sense, and Julia decided it would be safer not to dwell on the subject. There was, after all, a more pressing reason for her presence at Honeywell that evening, and time was running out on her with every passing second.

'Would you——' Her voice broke embarrassingly, and she had to steady her glass of sherry with both hands while she fought to regain control of her vocal chords. 'Would you have left on Monday without saying goodbye?' she managed eventually.

Nathan did not alter his sprawling position on the padded armchair. To someone who did not know him he might have appeared relaxed, but Julia was alerted to a certain tension in him which made her suspect that every muscle in his long body was flexed and ready for whatever action might be required of him.

'Would it have mattered?' His compelling glance drew hers and challenged her to reveal the truth. 'Would it have mattered to you if I had left Doornfield without saying goodbye?' He repeated his question when she hesitated to answer him.

'Yes.' She swallowed convulsively, her nerves strung as taut as the leather thongs on the seat of the antique bench against the wall behind him, but her glance did not waver from his. 'It would have mattered very much.'

'Why?'

His abrupt query seemed to hover in the air between them, challenging her and warning her simultaneously. She dared not deviate now. He was giving her the opportunity she had been seeking from the moment she had arrived, and she would be a fool to let it pass.

'I wouldn't have had the opportunity to—to tell you how much I hate myself now for—for what I did to you five years ago.' The words pouring so haltingly from her lips were not the words she had rehearsed with such care, but that did not seem to matter now. It was important that he should be told the absolute truth, and that was what she intended to do. 'You said the other night that—that I had had no right to—to make a decision on your behalf and, after a great deal of soul-searching, I find that I have to agree with you, but five years ago my decision was based on the fact that I—I cared too much to want to stand in the way of your success.'

She was in danger of spilling the contents of her glass into her lap, and she disposed of it hastily to gesture despairingly with her hands when a look of sceptical disbelief flashed across Nathan's face.

'Oh, I know this must sound like a weak excuse to you,' she went on doggedly, 'but I couldn't leave my grandmother when I knew she needed me, and I couldn't allow you to throw away the chance of furthering your skills as a neuro-surgeon. I know what your reaction would have been if I had confided in you. You would have insisted that I marry you, and perhaps I might even have succeeded in persuading you to go to Europe, but very few marriages would survive a three-year separation. It would have affected your work and your studies, and I didn't want that. I wanted you to be free to go and do what I knew you had always longed to do.'

'So you jilted me in writing and promptly disappeared, taking your grandmother with you.'

'Yes,' she nodded, the agonising memory of that hasty flight out of Johannesburg as fresh in her mind as if it had happened the day before. 'I couldn't face you and lie to you. I was afraid that you would make me change my mind, and I was afraid that if you chose to stay with me rather than furthering your studies you might reproach me in time for having lost that opportunity.'

Nathan's face hardened, but, despite the stubborn glint in his eyes, she knew that she was achieving credibility when she saw that tiny nerve pulsing along the side of his jaw.

'The decision would have been *mine*, Julia, and I would never have reproached you.'

'Not openly, no, but deep down in your heart you might have felt it,' she argued gravely. 'Resentment has a nasty way of building up stealthily inside one, and I couldn't have tolerated a barrier like that between us.'

Nathan lapsed into a silence which was disturbed only by the sound of the rain lashing against the windows. His frowning glance was directed at the tip of his suede shoes, and Julia was beginning to shift uncomfortably on her chair when he looked up unexpectedly to capture her wary glance.

'I take it that Damian has always known the reason behind your decision not to marry me?'

'Yes, he knew,' she confessed nervously. 'I went to him for advice, but in the end it was a decision only I could make.'

'I appreciate your honesty and, much as I hate to admit it, your argument makes sense to me now that I'm no longer caught up in a blind fury, but that doesn't eradicate the fact that I went to hell and back after you broke off our engagement.'

Nathan's cold, detached manner chilled her, and the accusation in his voice made her wince inwardly when it stabbed at wounds which had never quite healed over the years.

'So did I,' she croaked, 'if that's of any consolation to you.'

Nathan swallowed down the remainder of his drink,

the reading lamp beside him accentuating the plains and hollows of his ruggedly handsome features, and her heart twisted painfully in her breast when he got up unexpectedly to draw aside the curtains at the sliding glass doors. He stood with his back to her, and he seemed oblivious of the flash of lightning which forked across the night sky. The house shuddered on its foundations during the ensuing clap of thunder, and endless minutes seemed to elapse before he turned and pinned her to her chair with an incredulous look in his blue eyes.

'You're the most unselfish and self-sacrificing person I have ever known,' he said, combing his fingers uncharacteristically through his dark hair and shaking his head, and the tight smile curving his sensuous mouth stabbed at her soul. 'God knows I'm grateful, Julia, but my gratitude takes second place to the anger and bitterness inside me.'

'I didn't come here expecting you to forgive me, Nathan, and neither do I want your *gratitude,*' she said stiffly, her insides rejecting that word as if it were the plague. 'I came because I knew I owed you more than the brief explanation which I gave you the other night, and I have only one more thing to say before I go.'

Her heart was thudding nervously and painfully in her breast, and her legs felt like jelly beneath the weight of her body when she rose jerkily to her feet, but her candid grey glance held his as she cast aside the final fragments of her pride.

'My feelings for you haven't changed,' she confessed, her voice almost too low and husky to be her own, 'and you were right when you said that it was much more than a physical thing for me when we made love that night, but I was terribly ashamed of myself the following morning. I'd allowed my emotions to dictate my actions, and I'd given Marcia no more than a fleeting thought. I hadn't doubted her when she told me that you were going to be married, and she had also made it painfully clear that she had so much more to offer you in the way of advancing your career. I thought that was what you wanted, and I was afraid that it might jeopardise your future if we saw too much of each other. That's why I insisted that it would be better for both of us if we stayed out of each other's way.'

There! I've said it! she thought with a strange sense of relief. Now, if you want to, you may do your worst!

Nathan was white-faced with anger, and the words seemed to explode from him with a savagery that made her tremble with something close to fear when he bridged the distance between them with a few long strides to tower over her menacingly. 'Did you think I had become so ambitious that nothing else mattered to me?'

'I'm sorry, but——' She searched his harsh features for some sign of softening, but his face was an inscrutable mask, and she spread her hands in a helpless gesture of despair. 'Five years is a long time, and people change.'

'People change, but not to such an extent!' he barked at her, the angry accusation in his eyes searing her soul. '*You* haven't changed, and you were prepared to step back once again in favour of someone who might advance my damned career as if *that* was the only thing of importance to you!'

He was standing so close to her that her sensitive nostrils picked up the faint but pleasing woody odour of his masculine cologne. She would have given anything at that momet to touch him and feel his strong arms holding her, but it was a longing which she had to suppress forcibly. She had virtually no pride left, but she was not going to lay herself wide open to the humiliation of his rejection.

'That wasn't the only reason why I would have stepped back,' she said dully, and her face was pale with the effort to still those agonising forces inside her. 'I thought that, if you were going to marry Marcia, you must love her and, under those circumstances, it was best to forget what had happened between us.'

'What about your own feelings?' he demanded harshly. 'Or do you relish the thought of making a martyr of yourself?'

'I didn't see it that way,' she protested with a measure of distaste. 'I simply wanted what was best for you.'

'I see.'

The atmosphere was heavily charged, and Julia was caught up in a wave of despair during the ensuing silence. She met Nathan's cold glance and found no sign of softening there, but she had told him the truth at last, and she could only hope that she would find some comfort in that knowledge during the long, empty years ahead of her.

'Thanks for the drink, and your time,' she said, her voice choked with unshed tears as she picked up her handbag and walked blindly from the room.

'*Julia!*' That harsh note of authority in his voice jolted her nerves and brought her to a startled halt before she reached the hall. 'Come here!'

She turned slowly to face him, and her honey-brown hair danced about her shouders when she shook her head in defiance of his command. 'I think we've said everything there is to say, and——'

'You can't leave here while that almighty storm is raging outside, so shut up and come here!'

His features were set in that harsh, unrelenting mask, but the coldness had left his eyes to be replaced by a burning, probing intensity. She walked towards him, obeying his command as if she had no will of her own, and she did not stop until she stood a little more than a pace away from him.

'If you think I'm going to let you walk out of my life again, then you're mistaken!' There was a frightening tightness about his mouth when he took her handbag from her and flung it on to a chair, but there was something in the deep resonance of his voice that ignited a tiny flame of hope inside her. 'We've wasted five years, and I blame myself for that as much as I blame you, but I don't intend that we should waste another minute of the future unless it is absolutely necessary.'

There was an ache in the back of her throat that would not go away, and she swallowed convulsively. 'You—you can't possibly still want me!' she whispered incredulously, her eyes misting with tears.

'It's much more than *wanting*, Julia, but we can't go on from there until we've cleared the air between us.'

His hand gripped hers, his touch instilling a little warmth into her cold heart as he led her towards the sofa and drew her down beside him, but her mind remained wary and suspicious. Dear God, she prayed silently, staring down at that lean, sun-browned surgeon's hand which was still holding hers. Please don't let him do this to me if he doesn't really mean it! Please, God!

'I was determined to forget you,' he explained, his voice low and throaty, and tinged with anger. 'For five years I tried to make myself believe that I hated and despised you, but I never quite succeeded, and I was shocked to discover the extent of my failure that day when Marcia's reckless driving forced you into the ditch to avoid a collision.'

'I had the edge on you,' Julia felt compelled to

confide in him, and she could not quell that quivering expectancy which rose like a tide inside her when she looked up to glimpse a certain warmth in his eyes. 'I'd heard from Tant Sophie Breedt that you would be the new owner of Honeywell, and I was more or less prepared for the possibility that we might bump into each other again.'

'Anger and bitterness had made me draw my own conclusions as to why you had changed your mind about marrying me, and the desire to lash out at you dictated my abominable behaviour.' He shook his head and smiled wryly. 'Damian was right when he predicted that I would hate myself for it.'

She nodded, remembering that night when the two men had almost come to blows because of Nathan's accusations, and she dared to question him for the first time. 'Did you ever discuss marriage with Marcia?'

'Never!' His brows drew together in an angry frown. 'She was simply one of the many women I have know these past five years, but marriage to any one of them never entered my mind.'

Julia jerked her hand from his and gestured distastefully. 'Please, I—I don't think I——'

'I know you don't like what I'm saying,' he interrupted her firmly, 'but it's important to me that there must be complete honesty between us.'

'I—I'm sorry,' she stammered ruefully, and she clasped her hands tightly in her lap, steeling herself for whatever was to follow. 'Please go on.'

Her heart quickened to an erratic pace when he brushed his knuckles lightly against her cheek, then he rose abruptly to pace the floor as if he himself did not relish the thought of what he had to tell her, but, as he had said, there had to be complete honesty between them.

'My relationship with Marcia should have ended a long time ago, but I dare say I still found it flattering to my ego to have her around,' he explained in a clipped voice. 'I was going to talk to her after you and I spent that night together, but I changed my mind when you were so insistent about shutting me out of your life. I decided that it might be to my advantage to use Marcia in an attempt to gauge your true feelings, and that was why I didn't discourage her the last time she telephoned to say that she was driving up to spend a couple of days here on the farm.'

'That wasn't very nice of you.'

'No, it wasn't, but I was getting pretty desperate.' He halted his restless pacing, and his mouth curved in a mirthless smile. 'I also have another confession to make. It wasn't an accidental meeting that brought Marcia and me to Roland's home that Sunday afternoon when you were visiting Elizabeth. I had seen your car parked in the street outside their house, and I made it my business to bump into Roland at the hospital. Afterwards it wasn't very difficult to get him to invite us to his home for tea. I was hoping that I would learn something from your expression when you saw Marcia and me together, but you hid your feelings so cleverly that I was furious with you for dooming to death what I had considered an excellent plan of action.' His glance sharpened and lingered intently on her face. 'Why are you smiling?'

She had been unaware that she was smiling, but her expression sobered when she rose with an aching need to be closer to him. 'You don't realise what an effort it was to stay there and pretend that nothing was wrong.'

'Perhaps it might appease you to know that I felt the same.' His smile was derisive when she paused less than a pace away from him. 'I was beginning to know the feeling of defeat, but later in the week I decided that I couldn't let the matter ret there. The purpose of my trip to Johannesburg on Wednesday was to settle with Basil Grant the unfinished business of rejecting his offer. I also paid Marcia a visit, and I won't go into detail about the unpleasantness of that confrontation, but suffice it to say that that part of my life is over and done with at last.' He moved his wide shoulders as if he was shaking it off physically, and his mouth tightened with a hint of anger which she suspected was not directed at her entirely. 'I was in a feverish haste to see you when I arrived back in Doornfield. I needed a couple of straight answers to a few pressing questions, but I was totally unprepared for the shock of discovering the actual truth.'

The memory of his savage reaction to her confession was still terrifyingly fresh in her mind, and a shiver raced along her spine as she turned from him and lowered her eyes to the Persian rug beneath their feet. 'I'm inclined to think that I deserved your anger, but where do we go from here?'

'I want you,' he said, taking her firmly by the shoulders and swinging her round to face him. 'If it's at all possible, then I want you now more than I've ever wanted you before.'

She stiffened beneath his hands. 'Are you asking me to live with you?'

'I love you, Julia. I have never ceased to love you and need you, and that's what I've been wanting to tell you ever since we spent that night together.' His voice was vibrant with an emotion she had not believed she would hear again, and it was there in his eyes when he took her face between his hands and tilted it up to his. 'I'm asking you to marry me, and I swear I shall hound you day and night until I get an affirmative answer.'

An incredible warmth invaded her heart and filled her soul with a singing joy, but there was also a weariness deep inside her. It felt as if she had travelled a long, dreary road to find again the peace and inner tranquillity of that haven which she had been forced to reject so long ago, and now there was no reason for her to leave it ever again.

'Oh, Nathan!' she sighed, swaying towards him and smiling tremulously through the happy tears that leapt into her eyes. 'I love you so much, and I would marry you this very instant if it could be arranged.'

There was an odd tremor in his hands when he drew her closer still to the hard length of his body to claim her mouth in a kiss of such infinite tenderness that it touched her more deeply than anything had ever done before, but tenderness gave way to the escalating urgency of their emotions. The pain and suffering of the past was still very real, and they clung together, their arms straining with a need to be closer almost than their bodies would allow. Nathan's sensuous mouth trailed fire along her throat, but they sought each other's lips repeatedly with a hunger which refused to be assuaged.

The emotions clamouring through Julia were as fierce as the storm raging outside, and she was trembling uncontrollably in the circle of Nathan's arms when he finally eased his mouth from hers. His eyes were dark with desire, and there was a sweet, stabbing response inside her when she buried her flushed face against him where she could feel the roughness of his chest hair against her cheek. She could hear his heart beating as hard and fast as her own, and she was elated beyond expression at the knowledge that it was beating solely for her.

She sighed contentedly, her arms locked about his lean waist, but a niggling thought leapt into her mind seconds later. 'Would you have left on Monday without saying goodbye?'

'Of course not, you crazy woman.' He laughed mockingly, his warm breath fanning her temple. 'I was going to drive out to your cottage this evening, but you thwarted my plans once again. That's becoming quite a habit of yours lately, but I must admit that there was a certain therapy in watching you work your way nervously round to the actual reason for your visit.'

'So you enjoyed my misery, did you?' she demanded crossly, leaning back in the circle of his arms, and looking up into his amused face.

It was difficult trying to pretend that she was angry when she was not, and the laughter bubbling from her lips was stifled when Nathan's sensual mouth shifted over hers with an urgency that drew an eager response from her. His kisses affected her like a drug, making coherent thought impossible while he was edging her purposefully towards the sofa, and she was powerless to stop him when he lowered her on to it and held her there with the weight of his body.

'Tell me about Warren Chandler,' Nathan commanded without warning while his fingers deftly unbuttoned her blouse, and it sobered her to the extent that the flush of happiness faded on her face to leave her slightly pale.

'Warren was a good friend, and I shall always consider him as such,' she explained quietly and with a certain amount of sadness. 'He'd asked me to marry him, but I never had more to offer him than a platonic relationship, and I think he suspected that long before I actually put it into words the other evening.'

'I was insanely jealous of that man,' Nathan growled, brushing aside the silky material and sliding his hand possessively over her breast.

'And how was I supposed to feel about your relationship with Marcia?' she parried his statement, her pulse quickening beneath the erotic arousal of those probing fingers, and Nathan smiled twistedly.

'Were you jealous?'

'Yes, dammit, and you know it!' she laughed self-consciously, sliding her hands inside his shirt and loving the feel of his hair-roughened chest against her palms, but her expression sobered the next instant. 'Oh, Nathan!' she exclaimed, her voice choked as she flung her arms about his neck and buried her face against him. 'Have you ever wondered if you would make the same decisions and the same mistakes if you could have your life all over again?'

'I have often wondered that, and especially these past few days, but I'm not sure I've found the answer.'

'We've wasted so much time,' she sighed ruefully.

'Yes, we have,' he agreed, tipping her face up to his and kissing her warmly and satisfying on the lips. 'We'll take a drive into town in the morning to speak to Roland about releasing you, since we're going to be married as soon as I can arrange it, but right now I have something else in mind for us.'

There was a devilish glitter in his eyes when he got up and scooped her masterfully into his arms, and she did not need to be told what he had in mind when he carried her from the living-room and across the hall towards the long passage which led to the bedrooms.

'Are you in agreement, Julia?' he demanded throatily when he shouldered open the door to the main bedroom and kicked it shut behind them.

'Absolute agreement,' she murmured happily against his lips, the flickering fires of desire in his eyes finding an echo inside her.

There were still so many things to talk about, and so

many decisions to be made before he left on Monday to return to Johannesburg, but it could all wait. The long sacrifice had ended, and there was no sense in wasting this precious moment when fate had been kind enough to give them this second chance.

BRIGHT SMILES, *DARK* SECRETS.

Model Kristi Johanssen moves in a glittering world, a far cry from her small town upbringing.

She carries with her the horrific secret of physical abuse in childhood. Engaged to Philip, a top plastic surgeon, Kristi finds her secret a barrier between them.

Gareth, Philip's reclusive ex-film star brother, has the magnetism to overcome her fears.

But doesn't he possess a secret darker than her own?

Available July. Price £3.50

W●RLDWIDE

ROMANCE

Next month's romances from Mills & Boon

Each month, you can choose from a world of variety in romance with Mills & Boon. These are the new titles to look out for next month.

BENEATH WIMMERA SKIES Kerry Allyne
DEVIL AND THE DEEP SEA Sara Craven
FETTERS OF GOLD Jane Donnelly
A LIFETIME AND BEYOND Alison Fraser
FORCE OF FEELING Penny Jordan
ONLY MY DREAMS Rowan Kirby
LORD AND MASTER Joanna Mansell
A FLOOD OF SWEET FIRE Sandra Marton
EXCLUSIVELY YOURS Leigh Michaels
WHEN TWO PATHS MEET Betty Neels
THE CINDERELLA TRAP Kate Walker
BELOVED INTRUDER Patricia Wilson
PAINTED LADY Diana Hamilton
BITTER JUDGEMENT Elizabeth Power

Buy them from your usual paperback stockist, or write to: Mills & Boon Reader Service, P.O. Box 236, Thornton Rd, Croydon, Surrey CR9 3RU, England. Readers in Southern Africa — write to: Independent Book Services Pty, Postbag X3010, Randburg, 2125, S. Africa.

Mills & Boon
the rose of romance

Enjoy one beautiful romance after another this holiday.

A holiday provides the perfect opportunity to immerse yourself in a heady new affair and with the Mills and Boon Holiday Romance Pack you'll be spoilt for choice.

In this special selection you'll find four brand new novels from popular writers Emma Darcy, Sandra Field, Jessica Steele and Violet Winspear.

The collection is unique as well as being excellent value for money and will slip easily into your suitcase.

We think you'll find the combination irresistibly attractive.

Just like so many of our leading male characters.

Published July 1988. Price £4.80.

SPOT THE COUPLE
AND WIN A
£1,000
REAL PEARL NECKLACE
PLUS 10 PAIRS OF REAL PEARL EAR STUDS WORTH OVER £100 EACH

No piece of jewellery is more romantic than the soft glow and lustre of a real pearl necklace, pearls that grow mysteriously from a grain of sand to a jewel that has a romantic history that can be traced back to Cleopatra and beyond.

To enter just study Photograph A showing a young couple. Then look carefully at Photograph B showing the same section of the river. Decide where you think the couple are standing and mark their position with a cross in pen.

Complete the entry form below and mail your entry PLUS TWO OTHER "SPOT THE COUPLE" Competition Pages from June, July or August Mills and Boon paperbacks, to Spot the Couple, Mills and Boon Limited, Eton House, 18/24 Paradise Road, Richmond, Surrey, TW9 1SR, England. All entries must be received by December 31st 1988.

RULES
1. This competition is open to all Mills & Boon readers with the exception of those living in countries where such a promotion is illegal and employees of Mills & Boon Limited, their agents, anyone else directly connected with the competition and their families.
2. This competition applies only to books purchased outside the U.K. and Eire.
3. All entries must be received by December 31st 1988.
4. The first prize will be awarded to the competitor who most nearly identifies the position of the couple as determined by a panel of judges. Runner-up prizes will be awarded to the next ten most accurate entries.
5. Competitors may enter as often as they wish as long as each entry is accompanied by two additional proofs of purchase. Only one prize per household is permitted.
6. Winners will be notified during February 1989 and a list of winners may be obtained by sending a stamped addressed envelope marked "Winners" to the competition address.
7. Responsibility cannot be accepted for entries lost, damaged or delayed in transit. Illegible or altered entries will be disqualified.

ENTRY FORM

Name _____

Address _____

_____

I bought this book in TOWN _____ COUNTRY _____

This offer applies only to books purchased outside the UK & Eire.
You may be mailed with other offers as a result of this application.